# ANNIHILATION FROM HOME

# TERRENCE D. ASTLEFORD

AUTHOR'S NOTE:
This is a work of fiction. All names,
characters, places and incidents either are
the product of the author's imagination or
are used fictitiously, and any resemblance to
actual persons, living or dead, events, or
locales is entirely coincidental.

# PART 1
## DECEMBER 31, 2012
## NEW YEAR'S EVE

# CHAPTER 1

Opening the door, Sam enters the laboratory. Going in he looks over and notices the light on the answering machine blinking. Walking to the machine, he presses a button and it plays..."Dr... Ummm Sam... this is Tom... at Golden Excavation. We have found a very interesting set of bones... I think you would be interested in. Please call me back at 555-8745. This is very important that we talk... as soon as possible, beeeeep. That was your last message", a soft female voice says.

Hitting the end button, he picks up the phone and dials 555-8745 and waits for it to start ringing. On the third ring it is answered. A male voice on the other end says, "Hello. This is Tom, can I help you?"

"Hello, Tom... This is Sam Adring, returning your call. You said it was important?"

"Yes. Sam... We found what we think is an incredible find. We were at one of our regular excavations, when we ran across a set of bones... bones that I thought you would like to inspect?"

"Sure... Sure. Where can I pick them up?" he asks as he paces around the room as if he were nervous.

"We are having them delivered to you as we speak. You should receive them sometime before 3 today. If you don't, call me back and let me know. Okay?" Tom asks.

"Yeah... Sure Tom. Oh, and thanks for thinking of me", as he sits down and starts writing on a scratch pad.

"Hey... No problem Sam. Well, I gotta go. I have to be at our number 4-dig site in 2 hours. Let me know what you find, Okay?"

"You got it Tom. Talk to you later, and again... Thanks. I owe you one!" Sam says, as he hangs up the phone.

Picking it back up, he dials his wife's cell number, and waits. He sits down, as she picks it up on the second ring.

"Hello", she says.

"Hey babe... I just talked to Tom over at Golden!" he states to her.

"Yeah what did he have this time?" she asks as she remembers Tom always had something odd to ship to them.

"You won't believe this. He's sending us a set of bones... that he said they just uncovered at one of their sites. He sounded odd though", he says, trying to describe to his wife what he could tell from Tom's voice.

"What do you mean by odd, dear?" as she sounds somewhat confused.

"Well... he sounded like he wasn't supposed to be calling me... and was doing it without anyone else's knowledge. You know how Tom gets when he sends us bones he isn't supposed to?" he replies as he smiles to himself.

"Ahhhhhhh... I know exactly what you mean. I will be there in about an hour. Thanks for telling me dear", she says as she blows him a kiss on the phone.

"Kiss, kiss babe. See you in a little bit", he says as he hangs the phone up.

Walking to the door, Sam opens it and walks into the front desk area and talks to Amy... the receptionist. "Amy".

"Yes Dr... What can I do for you?" she asks as she smiles at him.

"If any packages come in today, would you let me know A.S.A.P... okay?" he asks like the gentleman that he is.

"Yeah, sure, okay Dr. Will there be anything else?" she asks, as sweet as can be.

"No, no. That will be all. Thanks Amy. You are a big help", he says, as he walks back to the lab and starts working on his latest experiment.

## Meanwhile at NASA...

"Hey, George", Paul says as he walks toward him.

"Hey Paul! What have you been doing lately? Haven't seen much of you around", he says as he grins.

"George. I have been fine. We need to talk about tomorrow's launch", as a serious look crosses Paul's face.

"Now, now Paul. We already talked about this… and we are going to have lift-off… tomorrow at 7:45 a.m. There is no way we are going to cancel……. because of what you think you have found," George says starting to get a little irate.

"But George. You know I'm right though. You can't deny what I have shown you. What would it take to prove it?" he asks as he fidgets around a little.

"You need substantial proof, Paul… Something concrete… We can't make any decisions on hearsay. Until you get something concrete, there's nothing I can do for you. If you can find anything… anything… you know anything that is rock solid. Some kind of proof other than your word" George says, as his tone softens up a little.

"Okay, George. But if something goes wrong, (as he raises his finger at him) you know I will be there to tell you, I told you so", Paul replies with a smile playing about his lips.

"Okay, Paul. I know you will. Hey I gotta go. I have a meeting I need to get to in about 5 minutes. Hey, tell the boys I said hi. Okay Paul?" George says.

"Okay, George. Tell the missy I said hi too. Hey, see you around George", he says, as he turns away and continues on his way to the launch pad.

"Okay. See you Paul", George says as he turns around and walks to the elevators.

## Meanwhile back at the lab...

Dr. Velma Adring pulls into the lot, and notices a delivery driver just pulling out of the lot. Smiling to herself she thinks.... It's here... as she gets out of her car and walks to the door. Walking into the building, she asks Amy," Is Sam in Amy?"

"Yes Dr. He's in the lab. The package just came and he said for you to go in their as soon as you came in", Amy says as she smiles.

"Okay. Thank you Amy", she says as she starts to walk to the lab door and then turns back around and says, "Oh Amy" she says as sweet as she can, " Can you get us some coffee please?" as she smiles.

"Sure Dr. I will be in with it as soon as I can. Now go", Amy says as she shoos her into the lab.

"You are a big help Amy. Thanks", she says, as she smiles and goes into the lab.

Closing the door behind her, she walks over to where her husband is at, and looks down on the table.  "Are these the bones Tom wanted us to look at?" she asks as she goes over to Sam and hugs him, then she looks up at him and they kiss quickly.

"Yeah, but look here" he points out. "These markings are all wrong. The bone structure is different too. Look here", as he points at the knee, "this isn't right. The bone should be much more inverted than it is here," he says sounding puzzled.

"And look here dear", as she points at the ribs, "The breast bone is much larger than any I have ever seen. And what is this", she says pointing at the third appendage and the tailbone.

"I don't know what we have, but I can guess… we are the only ones to ever uncover something like this", he says as he goes to a cabinet and gets out a bottle of dating acid.

Using a dropper, he sucks up some of the acid and drips it onto an area of bone to check the age of the bones. Sizzling as he pours it on, he closes the bottle and puts it away. Walking back, he scratches the bone with a surgical scraper where he put the acid and takes some samples. Getting his bone samples, he walks over to the microscope and looks at it. "What the…" he starts saying as he looks at it.

"What is it dear?"

"Come here and take a look", he says as he moves back from it.

Walking over to the microscope, Velma looks and is shocked at what she sees. "This can't be", she says with a puzzled look on her face. "This can't be possible… It has to be a mistake".

"I think we better analyze these more thoroughly… before we contact anyone", he says as he walks over to the bones and starts doing more tests on them.

Entering the lab with the coffee, Amy goes over to the desk and sets the coffee down. As she turns around, she sees the bones and says, "OOOOOhhh. What is that, a dinosaur?"

Looking at her, Sam raises his eyebrows and says, "Amy. You are brilliant. Vel, run me some DNA and RNA tests on them immediately. We need to see what they match up with".

"Okay. I will get my equipment and set it up. I will be right back", she says, as she looks at Amy and asks, "Could I bother you for some help Amy?"

"Sure Dr", she replies as he follows Velma out to her car.

While they are getting the equipment out of the car, Velma looks over at her and says, "So Amy. What do you have planned for this New Years'?" she asks as she starts gathering the equipment after locking her car up.

"I am going to go see my boyfriend, Nick. He has invited me over for a party he is throwing. He said it was going to be a blast. What are you two doing?" she asks back as she continues following the Dr. into the lab.

"I think we are going to be pulling an all-nighter tonight. This has got to be the biggest find ever. Oh, by the way. Will you transfer all our calls to the service, and you can go early today", she says, as she walks over to the oscilloscope and turns it on.

"Oh, Thank you Dr. you guys are the best ever. If I don't see you tonight, I will see you on Wednesday morning. You guys have a Happy New Years", she says, as she walks to the door and leaves.

"Okay. You too", she says, as she turns around.

Transferring the phones Amy walks out the front doors and locks them up with her key. She goes to her car, unlocks it and gets in. Starting it up, she heads home to get ready for tonight. Thinking about tonight, she smiles to herself and can only think about Nick. He has been such a great boy friend.  I can't ask for any better.... She thinks… Or any better looking.

## CHAPTER 2

Hitting the lights just right, she makes it home in record time. Pulling up in the driveway, she puts the car in park and shuts it off. She almost slips as she is getting out of the car. She walks up the steps to her front door and goes inside and starts getting her clothes ready for tonight. Laying her clothes out she notices her blouse is wrinkled. As she goes to the closet and gets the ironing board out, she hears a honk. Going to the window she looks out and sees Nick in his truck.

Leaning out the window he looks up at her and says, "Hey baby. Get off early today?"

"Yeah. They got some new bones in and I think they didn't want to be disturbed. Hang on, I will be right out", she says as she turns around and sets the ironing table up and walks outside.

Walking over to his truck he gets out and takes her in his arms and kisses her. Kissing him back she grabs his crotch playfully. "MMMmmm", he moans as they break from the kiss. "Better not do that. You know what will happen. We will never make it to the party", he says smiling sexily down at her.

"Okay", she says. "I will be good… Oh by the way. What time are you picking me up?"

"Oh. I almost forgot. We don't have to be at my place 'til 9:00 tonight. I told everyone else 9:30, but I would like to be there by 8:00 or 8:30 at the latest. You know how there are always people who get there early. I figure… I will be here at 7:30 to pick you up. Okay?" he asks.

"Okay. I will be ready" she replies smiling in her special way as she bats her eyelashes at him.

"Okay. I gotta go babe. I have a service call to go check on", as he kisses her bye and gets in his truck. Starting it up, he says, "See you at 7:00 or 7:30…Love you", as he blows her a kiss.

"Yeah. Same to you", as she smiles widely and waves.

Putting his truck in drive, Nick pulls away and waves as he is going down the road. Waving back, she walks back inside. Going into the spare room, she puts her blouse on the ironing board and then goes to the closet as she gets the iron out and plugs it in. Setting it on top of the dresser, she sets it for med. /cotton. Going to the kitchen, she fills the teapot up with water and puts it on the stove. Turning the stove on high, she turns and walks back to the spare room and checks to see if the iron is hot. Hearing the sizzle as she gets her finger wet and taps it quickly against the iron bottom, she starts ironing her blouse. Finishing that, she puts everything away and takes her clothes into the bedroom and sets them on the bed.

Hearing the teapot whistling, she goes into the kitchen and makes herself a cup of tea. Carrying it into her bedroom, she sets it down on the dresser and gets undressed. She walks into the bathroom and gets into the shower and turns it on. The water sprays out of the shower and is cold as it showers on her body. "Brrrrr", she exclaims as she turns the head away and gets the temperature right. She washes the day's dirt off her almost perfect body. She gets done and turns the water off. Grabbing her towel she dries herself off. Walking into the bedroom, she takes a sip of tea and catches a glimpse of herself in the mirror and then she starts doing a striptease act in front of it. Seeing herself, she starts laughing and falls down on the bed giggling.

As her laughter subsides, she gets up and starts getting dressed. After she is dressed, she looks at herself in the mirror and says to her reflection, "You are going to be the belle of the party".

Picking her tea up, she walks into the living room and turns on the television. As the picture starts coming in, she hears. "And in local news, the space shuttle Kennedy is all set for tomorrow's launch. Live at NASA headquarters at Kennedy Space Center is Jose Manuello"...the picture changes and goes to Jose at NASA..." Well Bill, we are live, with George Gregsin, head of launch command. George, so everything is set for tomorrow's launch, right?

George: Yes it is. We are proud to be launching the Kennedy.

Jose: George, we have a report, someone named Paul, who says this launch is doomed. Is this true?

George: No. There's no truth to this rumor that's going around.

Jose: George, what is the mission of this shuttle launch?

George: Well Jose, the mission this time, is to take a load of fuel and toxins that are needed to run the equipment up there. As you well know we have been experimenting with nuclear tools in space, because of the negative gravity effect. You see… up there, the toxins aren't as harmful. We don't breathe the air, or actually touch them. And from our studies, (as he scratches his head), show that in this way, we can help to rid our planet of these deadly toxins, by using them in a less stressful environment.

Jose: Is this shuttle going to have a crew aboard?

George: Yes. We would rather have a crew, than remote because of the payload involved.

Jose: Do you ever feel that this could be another Challenger or Columbia?

George: No. We feel those were just flukes. They were freak accidents. We at NASA feel that will never happen again. Well I have to go.

Jose: Okay. Thanks for talking with us George". The reporter turns around and faces the camera as he says, "And that was George Gregsin, the head of launch command for this particular lift off.

Clicking the television off Amy goes into the kitchen and makes another cup of tea. As she puts the kettle on the stove and turns it on, someone knocks on the door. "Coming", she yells as she heads to the front door. Opening the door she sees it is her neighbor, Laura Jiminy. Seeing who it is, she says, "Hi Laura. What brings you over here today?"

"I was just wondering if you and Nick were doing anything tonight?" she asks.

"Yeah... Don't you remember? Nick's throwing a party at his place tonight... Why? Weren't you guys invited?" Amy asks.

"Oh yeah. That's right. I did forget. I don't know if we were invited", she says, as she starts biting her fingernail.

"Well, if you aren't invited, consider yourself invited now", Amy says smiling. "Come on in", she invites.

"No... I can't. If we are going to the party, I better get ready... huh?" she replies as she smiles.

Amy looks at her watch and sees it is 6:45. "Damn. Where does the time go? I need to go freshen up. He's going to be here in a few minutes. Sorry to chat and run, but I do need to go and you need to get ready. If you need a ride, call me on my cell phone. You have the number, right?"

"Yeah. I have it. Okay. See you later Ames", she says, as she turns around and heads down the steps.

"Okay. See you tonight", Amy replies, as she goes inside and heads for the bathroom.

Turning on the light, she checks her make-up and sees that it is all right. Fluffing her hair up, she turns the light off and goes into the kitchen and makes sure everything is turned off and in order. Finding nothing wrong, she goes to the front door and turns on the outside lights. Grabbing her coat from the closet, she puts it on and closes the closet door. Walking over to her front door, she turns around gives one last look over her shoulder before walking out the front door and locking it. Walking over to the porch swing she turns around sits on the swing as she waits for Nick to show up. Thinking about Nick, she smiles. I can't wait 'til we are married...she thinks to herself. Just then, he pulls in and fishtails into her yard yelling out, "YEEEEEEHAWWWWWW", as he slams on the brakes to keep from hitting the tree. Parking his truck, he gets out and she goes running to him. Grabbing her up in his arms... they kiss. After they break apart, she hits him lightly and says," Just look what you have done to my yard".

"Hey baby. I'll fix it. You know that", he replies as he smiles and picks her up and kisses her again.

"I know", she says, as he picks her up.

Breaking apart he asks, "So are you ready to... PARTY?

"Hell yeah! Let's go", she says.

Opening the door for her, Nick helps Amy into his truck. Running around and getting in, he starts the truck up and says, "Watch this. I just had a new turbo charger put on today", as he revs the engine. They both put their seatbelts on and he says, "Ready?"

"Ready", she replies.

"Okay here we go", he says, as he lets off the brakes and jams on the accelerator and floors it.

Coming out of the yard the truck bounces over the edge of the roadway and the tires squeal when they hit pavement. As he turns out of her driveway, the truck fishtails to the left as he spins the wheel to the left and then tries to straighten it up. Shifting into second gear, the tires squeal again as he burns some rubber. Hitting a switch, the truck jumps forward so fast, it forces her into the seat. Laughing like a lunatic, he flips the switch off and steps on the brake lightly and says, "What do you think?"

"You are about the craziest guy I have ever been with", she says as she laughs.

# CHAPTER 3

Back at the lab, Sam and Velma are making some very extraordinary finds. After running her DNA and RNA tests, she says, "Sam. This isn't right. It's coming out that these are related to the dinosaurs of earth. I have never heard of any tri-pedal creature that ever lived here. At least, not that looks like this".

"I know Vel. Something's wrong. I can't place it, but all the tests I have been running don't figure right with what I have come up with. This... creature has all the configurations to belong to the dinosaurs... But... They only date back 20,000 years. That's not right", he says, as he continues running tests on the bones.

"Everything I come up with also figures wrong. For example when I ran a series of tests, they all came up with the same thing. The tests say it is only 20,000 years old too. There is no record of these bones anywhere in history. I think we have something here that is bigger than we think", she says as she sounds nervous and excited.

"Yeah. But what does it mean Vel? Are there creatures out there that we don't know anything about?" he asks with a serious expression on his face.

"It sure is beginning to look that way", she replies.

"I'm going to call John", he says, as he goes over to the phone.

"And what is he going to be able to tell us?" she asks, in a sarcastic tone.

"You know as well as I do that John knows a lot about bones from when he was a professor at the college in Georgia. I think he can shed some light for us", as he looks at the phone starts dialing the number.

"Okay. I won't argue…" she raises her finger at him and continues… "If you think that is right, I will agree with you", she says as she smiles at him.

Smiling back, he hears a man answer the phone, "Hello".

"John?" Sam asks.

"Yes. This is John… a pause and then… Sam… is that you?" he asks back.

Sitting down Sam says, "Yes John! The reason I called… Well we need someone with experience in tracing some bones to the proper period… but they have us stumped. Our tests indicate they are only 20,000 years old. And they are tri-pedal", he says as he tries to explain what they are without saying too much. "I just thought you might want to come on over and take a look".

"Yeah. I will be there shortly Sam. I'm leaving right now", he says. "I'll be there in about a half an hour."

"Okay. See you in a little bit then", Sam says as he hangs the phone up.

Walking over to the table with the bones on it, he says, "He'll be here in a few minutes Vel. I believe he will be able to tell us if these bones are even supposed to exist".

"I know Sam. I trust your judgement. I always have and always will", she says as she looks up at him and smiles.

Getting involved running his tests, Sam almost doesn't hear John knocking at the door. Going out to the door he sees John standing there as he unlocks it and opens it up. As John steps through the front door he says, "John. Come on in. Nice to see you again", as they shake hands.

"Same to you Sam. So, where are the bones you wanted me to look at?" he asks.

"Right this way John", Sam says, as he leads the way into the lab after locking the front door up and cautiously looking around outside the window.

Entering the lab, they go over to the table where the bones are and John looks down and his eyes open wide as he says, "This can't be right Sam. There are no tri-pedal creatures like that in any of our history. And you said it dated back only 20,000 years?"

"Yeah. That was it. Do you know anything about them John?"

"No. I have never seen or even heard of anything like this at all. Where did you get these from?" he asks Sam.

"A friend of mine…"he pauses briefly… "Sent them down from one of his sites", Sam replies looking kind of confused.

"I need to know exactly where these bones came from. Can you call him and find out?" John asks.

"Yeah. Sure. Hold on a minute, let me see if he's on his cell phone", Sam says as he walks over to the phone and dials up Tom's cell number. Hearing it ring… he smiles and waits. On the fourth ring, Tom answers, "Hello".

"Tom. This is Sam. I need to know where these items are from. Sam asks.

"Yeah. They came from a dig we have in South Carolina. We got them at the bottom of an old mine we had there, about 3,000 feet down", he says as he sips his drink.

"John. He says they came from South Carolina from a mine of theirs. About 3,000 feet down he said. Is that all?" he asks, as he holds his hand over the mouthpiece.

"Yeah. That's all I need to know. Thanks Sam."

"Okay", he says, as he takes his hand off the phone and says, "Thanks Tom. That's all I needed. Oh and by the way… Happy New Years to you and yours", as he stands up.

"Okay. Anytime Sam… Same to you and the missus… Talk to you later", Tom says as he hangs the phone up.

As he hangs the phone up he goes over by John and asks, "So what do you make of it now?"

"These are unbelievable. There is no way they would be 3,000 feet down… and only be 20,000 years old.  That's impossible", John says shaking his head.

"So what do we do now?" Sam asks, looking at Velma and shrugging.

"I don't know. I say we should study them and see what we can find out. Come on let's get to work.  Velma, we need a couple of saws and maybe 4 syringes with a #10 needle", John says, as he starts dismantling the creature.

"Okay. I'll be right back", she says.

Leaving the lab and going into the storage room, she gets the things John asked for and brings them back to the lab. Setting them up, she has everything to begin with whatever John has in mind. Looking over at them, she sees John has taken some ribs out and is showing Sam something. Sam is shaking his head in agreement as she walks over to them and sees what they are doing. Looking down at the table, she hears John say, "Sam. Look here", pointing his finger at the ribcage. "When you take these 2 bones out, if you look real closely, you can see they never went there to begin with. There are no attachment places for the bones to go there. I think something is fishy here Sam", John says, as he shakes his head, trying to figure out what the hell is going on.

# CHAPTER 4

Arriving at Nick's house, after showing off his new stuff, he pulls into his yard and does a couple of donuts as he shreds up some grass. Laughing like a lunatic, he stops the truck and takes his keys out of the ignition and goes around to Amy's side of the truck and helps her out. Not letting her feet touch the ground, he carries her up to the porch. Unlocking the door, he kicks the door open and carries Amy inside. Leaving the door open, he puts her down and kisses her. Taking her hand he leads her into the kitchen and says, "I wasn't sure what to get, or how many people there were going to be, so I just bought a whole bunch of different stuff".

"It looks like you've thought of everything. Oh… I bet you forgot to get champagne", she says smiling at him slyly with a slight twinkle in her eye.

Opening a door beside him, he says, "Wallah". Stacked inside, are about 25 bottles of champagne. He starts laughing and says, "And here, I thought you had faith in me", as he laughs a little harder.

"I do and you know it", she says, as she hits him in the arm playfully.

"Knock, knock", they hear from out front.

Going to the front door, they see Nick's neighbor standing there with a bottle of Whiskey and some sweet and sour mix. Smiling, Nick says, "Hey Lewis. You didn't have to bring that", as he smiles.

"I know. I just thought you might want to have a few drinks with me. Hi Amy. Long time no see", Lewis says, as he walks in and hands the bottle to Nick.

Kissing Amy on the cheek, Nick takes Lewis into the kitchen and gets out a couple of glasses. "Amy" he holler's.

"Yeah", she replies.

"Do you want a whiskey sour, extra sour?" he asks as his hand hovers near a glass.

"Yeah. I would like that and thanks", Amy says.

Grabbing another glass, he proceeds to make the drinks. After he is done, he takes 2 and lets Lewis get his own. Walking out to the front, Nick hands Amy a drink and then walks into the living room and turns the stereo on. Walking to the front closet he opens the door and turns the switch on as the front and sides of the house light up. Closing the box he closes the door and goes out front and sees that Fisher and Charlie have shown up. Going over to them, he sticks his hand out and says, "Hey Fishman. What's up?"

"Not a lot Nick... you?" as he shakes his hand.

"Just having a good time, that's all", as he turns to Charlie and sticks his hand out and says, "Chuckie buddy, (seeing as how Nick is the only one that can get away with calling him Chuckie, as he saved his life). Where the hell have you been? On vacation! I have a shit-pile of scraps I need you to haul away for me", Nick says, as he shakes his hand.

Shaking Nick's hand back, Charlie says, "No. I've been rather busy lately. Seems everyone has stuff to haul away now. So, what's been happening with you?" he replies.

"Not a lot. Working harder than ever though. It seems like everyone wants to have A/C this year. I guess it is popular this year, huh Chuckie?" as he pokes him in the ribs laughing.

Laughing with him Charlie says, "Yeah... Just like junk", as he burst out in a new fit of laughter.

"Yeah. I thought junk was a year round job their Chuckie?" Nick says, as he laughs again.

Charlie laughs along with him. Coming up the steps are Stu and Laura. Walking to the top of the porch, Nick sticks his hand out and says, "Stu you dog", as Stu shakes his hand back.

Holding his arms out, he says, "Laura-a-a-a...Long time no see", as he hugs her and she hugs him back, though she is thinking.... God I hate this guy. I wished him and Stu had never met... as she smiles.

"So, what are you good people up to?" Nick asks.

"Just coming here to have a great time. Got anything to drink?" Stu asks, as he smiles.

"Of course I do. You know that. You know where it is. Please... Help yourself", Nick says, as he walks them inside.

As they enter, Nick says in a melodramatic way, "Everyone. This is Stu.... And his lovely if not beautiful wife, Laura", moving out of the way, so everyone can greet them.

HAHAHAHAHA... Nick thinks as he goes out front, where he finds Amy, sitting on the swing. "Hey babe. What's up?" he asks, with a concerned look on his face.

"Nothing. Just wondering when we are going to spend some time together again. Every time I turn around you are talking to someone else... Or you are in the kitchen with George... Or you are too busy working all the time", she says, as a tear rolls down her cheek. Wiping the tear away, Nick takes her face in his hands and gently caresses it saying ever so lightly, "It's my party babe. I have to at least greet the people. As for working all the time, you must be thinking about yourself... not me. I am always home by 7:00 at night. You are the one who gets up at 5:00 a.m. and then you don't get home 'til 9 or 10 at night".

Wiping her tears away, she says, "Well. I just want to start spending some time with you. We are engaged and we see each other what....... One night a week?"

"Okay. After tonight I will make time for you... (as he pauses)... if you make time for me", he says smiling slyly.

"Okay… I can do that", as a smile comes to her lips.

Looking down at her, he pulls her closer and kisses her fully on the mouth. Kissing him back, she wraps her arms around his neck. Breaking away, Nick asks, "So, are you all better now?"

"Yeah. Here are some more people", she says, as headlights come down the street and slow down.

Getting up, Nick walks over to the stairs and waits for the people. Driving in, they park next to Nick's truck. Noticing whose car it is, Nick knows that it's Fran, Bill and Joan carpooling it again, as usual. Shutting the engine off, they get out and Nick starts laughing as Fran stumbles out of the back and falls face first, into a fresh pile of dirt, (from when Nick did donuts coming in). Trying to hold his laughter in, Nick bursts out, and is soon sitting on the steps, as he can't seem to quit laughing. Looking up, Fran says, "Hey, you freakin' asshole. Shut the hell up. It's not my fault", as she gets up and goes inside to use the bathroom to clean up.

Nick feeling bad follows Fran into the house. "Fran wait", he says as he stops her just outside the bathroom door. "I'm sorry Fran. I didn't mean to…"

She looks at him and stops him as she says, "It's all right. I probably would have laughed at me too", as she bursts out laughing and he joins her. "Hurry up", he says as he starts off to the front of the house and thinking of Amy as usual.

Pretty soon, everyone is laughing and the party is going in full swing. At 11:30, Nick hears the rumble of a hog. Looking out the window, he sees his good friend, Dude just pulling in. Smiling to himself, he heads for the door and goes out. Walking down the stairs, he approaches Dude and says, "Hey, Dude bud. What the hell are you doing? I thought you were up in New York?" Nick asks questioningly.

"Hey, Nick... Yeah I was up there for awhile, but the work ran out and now I'm down here", as they exchange a bikers handshake.

"Come on in Dude. This party is going to last all night. I'm going to watch the shuttle take off tomorrow morning. And you... Can you handle staying up all night?" Nick asks, as they walk into the house.

"I can handle it. I have stayed up all night more times than I can remember. Hey where the hell is the beer at?" he asks, as he burps and Nick smells beer on his breath already.

"In the fridge. You know where it is. Help yourself", he says, as he walks into the living room and turns the 52" big screen on, so they can watch the ball drop in Times Square. As Dude comes back from the kitchen, Nick finds Amy and takes her into the kitchen. "Come on Ames. We need to get the champagne in glasses. Then we have to get it set out for everyone out there", he says, a little bit frantically, cause he forgot.

"I've already poured it and it's out on the table. If you would just notice the things I do once in a while. I swear... But I love you anyway", she says as she smiles at him and leads him out to the living room, where he says, "Champagne is in here. Come and get a glass and hurry, we only have 1 minute left", he says as Amy leads him to a dark corner.

At 11:59:45, everyone has their champagne, and as the countdown begins, everyone counts with it..."Ten... Nine... Eight... Seven... Six... As someone shouts out, "YEEHAWW" ... Two... One... HAPPY NEW YEARS", as they all shout. People are hugging each other, and others are kissing, and yet others are engaged in conversation.

When the countdown was over, Nick and Amy raised their glasses, and he said, "To you, my love. May we always be together and make each other happy. This is to you, my only love", and she says, "And to you also, for being there and putting up with all my craziness. To you, my only love", and then they clink their glasses and they gulp it down. Throwing his glass away, (everyone hears it break), he takes her in his arms and kisses her deeply.

Throwing her glass at the same time, she kisses him back and they are stuck that way, it seems for 25 minutes. "Hey everyone. The host is getting some over in the corner", someone yells out and someone else points a spotlight at them.

Turning red, they both start laughing as everyone else does to as they run up the stairs to his bedroom. They enjoy the rest of the evening with each other. No one even bothers to disturb them.

# CHAPTER 5

Crunching some of the bones up, John starts running tests of his own on them. Running around the lab like a chicken with its head cut off, he just goes from test to test shaking his head. Mumbling under his breath, he approaches Sam and says, "Every test we have run... comes back with the same thing. But that's impossible", as he shakes his head in frustration.

"I know. I can't believe it either. So what do you make of it?" Sam asks.

"I'm starting to think things that would make sense, but no one wants to hear", he says with a frightened look on his face.

"John... What are you talking about?" Sam asks.

"I'm talking about us even being from here... Now wait a minute and hear me out", he says as he sees John about to say something. Then you can say I'm crazy. Here's what I think. I think we are not even from this planet, but from somewhere else. I think we were transplanted from somewhere else, by some kind of advanced civilization. And... I think they didn't know this body was there. Everything I have ever studied now makes total sense. Now it all comes together. But my question is who would do that and why? And where are they?" John asks with as he looks at both of them with a stern and serious look on his face.

"John... I see where you are coming from. I see exactly what you are saying. And yes, it does make sense. Hey, what about you Vel? Doesn't everything you have ever learned, seem to fit right in with the picture we have here... before us?" Sam asks.

"Yes. I do have to agree with you two. It all really does make sense. As for your questions John, I have no theory or explanation", Velma replies.

"Sam... We've got to tell someone. We can't keep it a secret", John says, as he goes toward the phone.

"Hold on a minute there, John", he says. "First, we better run some more tests, just to be sure. You know, once we say something... the government is going to come in here and no one will ever know what we found".

"You may be right there, Sam. Okay. How about tomorrow morning, we go to the papers and show them what we have, and see if they will print a story about it, before we tell anyone, so no one can cover it up", John suggests.

"Yeah. I agree with you John. Let's do that. Okay first we need to get all the bones together, with the photo's we have. We need to take all our papers, with our notes on them, "Sam says giving orders, as they all gather up the bones and papers.

Carrying all the stuff down to the garage, they load up the van that belongs to the labs. Locking the van up, John says, "I'm going to stay and watch it. You guys go on up, and turn everything off and lock up. I will make sure someone doesn't know about this… already".

"Okay. Come on Vel. We'll be back in 5 minutes", Sam says, as they leave and go back to lock up the building.

Coming back, John is still waiting. Smiling as he walks over, Sam says, "So, where do we go for now?"

"I think we should go to the local newspaper offices, and see if anyone there can give us some information, as to when we can talk to a reporter. Then, if one isn't available for a while, we will go somewhere and wait", John says.

"Okay. Let's do it", Sam says, as he starts the van up and puts the van in reverse. Backing up, he shifts into neutral, then drive and drives out of the garage. Exiting the building, they head down the dirt road, and as they approach the main road they turn left. Going down Old Tampa Highway, they take it to the end, (Airport Road), and turn right. They take that to Bermuda Avenue and head north. As they enter the town, they turn right on Emmett St. and then they go the local newspaper offices and pull in. Getting out of the van, John goes up to the door and looks in the window.

Looking on the window, he sees they will be closed tomorrow for New Years Day. "Damn", he says to himself. He turns around and walks back to the van with a disappointing frown on his face. "They are going to be closed tomorrow for New Year's", he says, as he gets into the van.

# CHAPTER 6

As a New Year begins, Nick walks around and sees almost everyone sleeping. He looks over, and Dude is fast asleep on the sofa, with Fran lying on top of him. Must have been a hell of a party, Nick thinks to himself. Stepping over Fisher, who happens to be passed out on the floor, Nick goes into the kitchen and makes a pot of coffee. As the coffee starts brewing he goes outside and looks at the tracks he made last night. As he is looking at them, he starts laughing, as he remembers Fran, falling down in the dirt. He starts laughing out loud, when he can't seem to control it any longer.

Just then, Amy came out and said, "What the hell are you doing, you fool?"

"I was just remembering last night, when Fran fell down in the dirt", he says, as he continues to laugh.

"Have you been up all night babe?" she asks, as she goes over to him and hugs him.

Hugging her back, he replies, "Yeah. But if I don't want to work, I don't have to. That is the benefit of owning your own business", as he starts laughing again.

"What time is it anyway?" she asks, as she looks on her wrist and finds her watch gone.

"It's 6:45 a.m. In just one hour, they are going to launch the newest shuttle. The Kennedy", he says, all excited.

"I heard about that. So, let's get some coffee going", Amy says, as she starts dragging him into the house, headed for the kitchen.

"I am way ahead of you babe. I already have a pot brewing... right now", he says in a smart aleck tone as he smiles.

"MMMmmm, I can smell it already".

Laughing together, they run up the steps and into the house, jumping over Fisher, just in the nick of time. As Nick's foot comes down, Fisher looks up and mumbles something, before lowering his head to the floor again and passes out.

As they enter the kitchen, they can smell the full force of the aroma of the fresh brewed coffee. Getting 2 cups out of the cupboard, Amy pours 2 cups of coffee and adds some sugar and cream to his. Stirring it up, she picks it up and hands it to Nick, as she says, "Here you go babe. Just how you like it", smiling sexily at him.

"Thanks babe", he replies as he takes a sip. "MMMMmmmmmmm", he moans to her.

"Is it all right?" she asks, raising her eyebrows.

"This is delicious", he replies as he smiles at her.

Walking out to the porch, Nick remembers something and says, "Oh shit!" as he sets his coffee down and runs into the house before Amy can say anything.

Setting down on the swing, Amy starts swinging, wondering what he forgot to do. Smiling... she thinks... that's my baby, always forgetting things... She laughs lightly to herself. Running to his bedroom, he has to jump over 3 people that are passed out on the floor. Finally as he gets to his room, he finds his video camera and goes back out to the front porch. Going down the steps she sees that he has his video camera again. Shaking her head she knows what he is about to do. She smiles and watches as Nick runs out back and she hears the roar of his boom truck come to life.

Hoping he doesn't wake anyone up, Nick gets the boom truck started and takes the video camera and puts it on his special camera mount. Making sure all the screws are tightened, he goes to the cab and jumps in. As he shifts into reverse he backs it out of the barn. As the truck clears the doors he cranks the wheel to the right. As he is turning the wheel back to the left with his left hand, he is depressing the clutch and shifting into first gear. It grinds slightly as it goes in and the truck moves forward with a jerky motion.

Driving out by the road, Nick parks in a certain spot, where he has the best view. Waving for Amy to come over she gets off the swing and grabs their coffee cups and takes them out to where he parked the truck. As she gets there he says, "Come on baby. Go up with me on this one? You will enjoy it... I promise", as he smiles and then gives her his best puppy dog eyes, that he knows she can't resist.

"Okay...I will... But only because you promise", she says, smiling at him.

Helping her into the bucket, Nick gets in and it starts to wiggle a little bit. Turning the key on, Nick starts the generator up and waits for it to start idling. Looking at her, he asks, "Are you ready for the time of your life?"

"I'm as ready as I will ever be", she replies.

"Here we go", he says, as the bucket starts going up.

As the bucket rises, Amy looks down and tries to grab hold of his arm, making the bucket rock. "Calm down babe. Take it easy", Nick says soothingly, trying to calm her down.

"Okay. I'll try to relax", she says, easing up on his arm.

Continuing up, they go about fifty feet before the boom stops extending out. Looking at his watch, Nick sees it is 7:40 a.m. and places his camera where he can see it, with nothing in his way. Reaching under the control panel, he removes his thousand to one zoom lenses for the camera. Attaching it to the camera he looks through the viewfinder and sets it to where he thinks it is going to go up. Turning a radio on they listen as they hear the announcer get ready to start the countdown to lift off. Listening to the announcer, Nick hears:

Announcer: We are here; live at Kennedy Space Center, where they will be launching the newest shuttle, 'The Kennedy'. In just a few minutes you will see live coverage as our cameras bring the whole thing… Live. We talked with George Gregsin earlier this morning. Here is a brief report as to what he said as they replay the earlier conversation. Turning the radio down, Nick says, "Well it's just about time", as he looks at his watch. Getting ready, he puts his eye to the viewfinder and waits… as he sees the time in the upper left corner of the camera. It is 7:44, and the countdown is just about to start, Nick thinks to himself. Reaching down he turns the radio up and hears the announcer's voice, saying the countdown. It is just at nine as he hears it continue... Eight … Seven... Six... Five... Four... Three... Two... One... We have ignition.

Looking through the viewfinder Nick gets ready. As the announcer says, "We have lift-off", Nick looks for the shuttle and finds it through the viewfinder. Zooming in it looks like he is right next to it. Following it up he sees it start to shudder and shake. Shaking his head, but still following it he says, "Oh my god Amy. There's something wrong with the shuttle!" he exclaims as he continues recording.

Watching it veer off course he follows the progress of the shuttle. It veers wildly off course as he hears the announcer on the radio saying, "Oh my god. The shuttle has gone off course and is pin wheeling about the sky… like a balloon with the air being let out. This is"... silence, as Nick turns the radio off and concentrates on the shuttle.

Following it, he watches as it veers over the Atlantic Ocean and starts heading out toward

Bermuda. All of a sudden, without any warning Nick watches as the shuttle blows up. Getting it all live on tape he sees the mushroom cloud as it spreads out across the landscape. Shaking his head he starts the generator up and starts taking the lift down. When they are halfway down, the bucket starts shaking violently as they feel the repercussion of the explosion. "WOW", Nick yells out.

Landing the bucket on the ground he gets out and helps Amy out. "What did you think babe?" he asks.

"I think it was great until the shuttle blew up", she said shaking lightly.

"Hey babe… Just be glad it's not me that was in there. We still have each other… don't we?" he asks pleadingly.

"Yeah. That we do. Thanks I needed that", she says as she smiles at him.

Nick turns around and goes back to the truck. Taking his camera off the mount he puts the lens back under the control box. Going over to Amy he hands her the video camera and goes over to the bucket and gets back in. Starting the generator up he lifts the bucket and lowers it into the special bracket that is mounted on top of the truck. Shutting the generator off Nick jumps out of the bucket and lands next to the driver's side door and gets in. As he starts the truck he puts it into gear and drives it over to Amy and motions for her to get in. Opening the door she gets in. Driving forward he drives around the back and pulls into the barn. Shutting the engine off, he gets out and goes around and helps Amy out as he smiles at her.

Smiling back she lets him help her out. Slamming the door shut he takes Amy's hand and leads her into the house. Going in they see everyone is up and drinking coffee. Running into the living room he turns on the television and says, "Hey everyone. The shuttle blew up today. I have it on video. Anyone want to watch?" he asks as he hears everyone say, "Yeah", in various stages of waking up.

Taking the tape out of his camera, Nick puts it into his VCR and rewinds it. Switching the surround on the tape stops and Nick pushes play. As everyone's attention is riveted to the set he narrates for his friends... telling them what he was thinking at the time. After watching it everyone starts talking at once. Turning the VCR off he turns the station to the local news where they are talking about it. Walking to the kitchen he goes in and makes himself another cup of coffee. Sipping it he knows that the shuttle is all anyone is going to be talking about... for weeks to come.

# PART 2
## JANUARY 1, 2013

# CHAPTER 1

Driving to Orlando John, Sam and Velma finally find a reporter they can talk to. Upon hearing their story and seeing their evidence he makes them wait, so they can talk to the editor himself. Waiting for what seems like hours they finally see the guy coming back with an older gentleman… who looks to be in his sixties? As they introduce themselves they explain everything to him and show him all the proof he needs. Telling them to wait he says he is going to get a couple of his best writers so they can tell them and they can then write the story. Coming back shortly with 2 more guys in tow, he introduces them. When they are all seated they explain again why they were there and proceed to tell them the whole story again… as the writers start writing. Showing them photos of the bones the way they were meant to be, the editor asks if he can keep it… for the front page and they say yeah. After all is said and done they take what they have left and return to the van. Looking at his watch Sam says, "In forty-five minutes, the shuttle will be going up. Anyone care to watch it with me?" he asks as he drives back to the lab.

"Yeah I will dear", Velma replies.

"I can't. I need to get home so Joan doesn't start worrying about me", John says as he yawns.

Pulling into the garage 30 minutes later they all get out and John says good-bye and that he will be seeing them later, as he leaves and goes out the garage door heading for his car. Going into the lab they put the stuff down on the table. Going over to the little television set in the corner Sam turns it on, without volume. Going into the office Velma makes a pot of coffee. Walking to the bathroom she turns on the light and goes in. Looking at his earlier tests, Sam shakes his head, not believing what they found out.

As Velma comes back in, she is carrying 2 cups of coffee. As she gets near him, she hands him one and looks over at the television. As she watches she sees the shuttle taking off and she says, "Sam honey. The shuttle is taking off".

"Thanks dear", he says, as he takes a sip of his coffee and watches as the shuttle goes up and then goes out of control. They both breathe in, as it explodes,
"AAAAAAAHHHHHHHHHHHH!"

"Oh my god", Sam says as a shocked look crosses his face.

"Noooooooooo", Velma cries out as tears come to her eyes.

Not believing it but having to Sam takes Velma in his arms and comforts her. "SHHHHHHH", he croons, as he holds her tight.

Shuddering as she sobs openly now, Sam does what he can to comfort her knowing her brother was the shuttle pilot and her only living relative. A fresh wave of shudders and crying ensue for hours as he comforts her in her time of need.

# CHAPTER 2

As she helps get everyone more cleared up and on their way, Nick and Amy start cleaning up. Finally, getting the house straightened up Nick takes Amy's hand and leads her to his bedroom. As he leads her in, he smiles wickedly. Smiling back, she knows what he wants. Leading her to the bed, they lie down in each other's arms and fall asleep. Awakening at 7:00 p.m., Nick wakes Amy up and asks if she would like to get a shower. She says yes, and goes in and starts the shower. Nick walks downstairs and starts a pot of coffee. Checking his voice mail, Nick sees if he has any calls. After hearing the voice tell him he has no new messages, he smiles and thinks... Thank god... As he mouths yeah, while balling his hand into a fist and bending his elbow and pulling it down as he mouths the words.

Hearing the shower running, Nick goes to the fuse box and shuts off the floodlights and turns on the regular lights, on the porch. Going into the living room, Nick turns on the television, and sees if there is anything new on the shuttle. Keeping the volume down, Nick watches to see if they show it. Finally hearing the shower cut off, he decides to give her five minutes before going up. Going out to the front porch, he sees something weird... in the sky. Turning the outside lights off he glances towards the east and sees a strangely odd green glow emanating over the horizon. I wonder what that is.... He thinks to himself.

Going in he walks to the bedroom and goes in. When he enters he sees her combing her hair. Smiling at him, she says, "It's all yours darling".

"Okay, thanks babe. Oh by the way. If you get a chance, go out on the front porch and look east and tell me if you see anything.... Umm..... Out of the.... Aaaa... Ordinary", he says.

"Okay", she says as they briefly kiss and he heads to the shower.

Walking out to the front porch, she takes a look and is struck with a bad feeling. She trembles slightly as she looks at it. Turning back around she goes back in and walks into the bedroom. Lying down on the bed she can hear Nick in the shower.

As she was walking out, Nick went into the bathroom and turned the shower on. Getting in, he washes his lean and muscular body. Lathering his hair up, he rinses his hands off. Rinsing the soap off his body, Nick rinses his hair out and conditions it. After rinsing the conditioner out of his hair, he turns the water off and dries off. Stepping out, he feels the cold tiles on his feet. Wrapping the towel around his waist, he goes into the bedroom. As he looks at Amy, he sees she is pale. Going over to her he asks, "Babe. Is everything all right?"

"Well. I went out there and saw what you were talking about and I started trembling as I looked at it. I also felt a strange feeling... Like it's a bad thing, Nick", she says, in a shaky, terrified voice.

"Shhhh, babe. It's all right. Don't worry. It will be fine", he says, as he tries to comfort her. Leading her into the living room, they sit down on the couch and watch the television.

Lying her head on his shoulder, he sees them talking about the green glow, so he turns up the television.

Announcer: We are coming to you live, from Miami Beach. As we look out over the Atlantic Ocean, (as the announcer turns around and looks as the camera pans over his shoulder and behind him), we can see a bright, green glow... emanating from it. We have reason to believe the shuttle had something to do with it. This green glow didn't appear until after the shuttle blew up. We have with us... a spokesman from a local radar station. Sir... Tell our viewers what your name is?

Mike: Hi. My name is Mike. Hi Mr. Nandy. I watch you all the time, as he giggles ever so slightly.

Mr. Nandy: What can you tell us about this green glow we are seeing in the Atlantic Ocean? Can you tell us what has caused it?

Mike: Well, from what I have seen, I have reason to believe it is the toxins... which probably evaporated into the ocean and is causing this

green glowing effect you see now. As far as I
know the green glow… well… it's because of
when the toxins entered the salt water... it created
a luminescence that is the green you see now.

Mr. Nandy: Can you tell us if it is safe to go into
the water? And how long could this last?

Mike: I would stay out of the water until the
EPA can run some tests and confirm that it is
okay to go in.  I figure… it will last anywhere from
a day... To who knows? My guess… could be a
week or two.

Mr. Nandy: Well, thank you Mike, (as he
shakes his hand).

Mike: Well you heard it all. What do you guys
at the studio think?

Studio: Well Bill, we haven't really thought
about it. But… I would say that guy probably
didn't know what he was talking about"... As they
all laugh.

Bill: Okay. Well, it's back to you in the studio.

The television is silent, as Nick mutes it.
Looking at Amy, he sees she is sleeping again.
Trying to pick her up without waking her, he
carries her into the bedroom and lays her on the
bed. Reaching over, Nick sets the alarm clock for
5:00. Lying down next to Amy he puts his arm
over her chest and falls asleep.

## CHAPTER 3

After taking Velma home and putting her to bed, Sam goes outside and breathes some fresh air in. Looking to the east, he sees a green glow and figures it is from the sun as it goes down. Walking inside he goes into the kitchen and makes him a cup of coffee. Walking over to the television he turns it on and then he goes over to the couch and grabs the remote as he switches to the news. He sees the news cast about the green glow and what that one guy in Miami had said. Switching the set off, Sam goes into the bedroom and wakes Velma up, shaking her gently and whispering in her ear.

Waking up, she blinks her eyes and asks in a sleepy voice, "Yeah honey, what do you want?"

Relating to her about the green glow that has since appeared, since the shuttle exploded. Telling her that he thinks something is not right he asks if she wants to go and see if John will fly them out there.  She begs off, saying she is not feeling good. Sam kisses her on the cheek and goes into the living room and calls up John. Picking up the phone on the second ring, he says, "Hello".

"John. This is Sam again. Have you been watching the news... or looked to the east lately?"

"No. As a matter of fact... I just woke up an hour ago. What about the east?" he asks Sam.

"Well... Ever since the shuttle blew up there's a green glow in the Atlantic Ocean... around where it went down", Sam replies as he fidgets around a little.

"A green glow?" John asks.

"Yeah. You can see it from here... As if it were close to us", he states.

"No! Why, what do you have in mind Sam?"

"I was just wondering if you could fly us out there and get a good look at it." Sam replies.

"I'm not sure about that Sam. What can we possibly gain by going out there and looking at a green glow in the ocean?" John asks sarcastically.

Hearing a knock at the door Sam says, "Hold on a minute. Someone's at the door", as he goes to the front door. Opening it he sees 2 guys dressed in black from head to toe. "May I help you?" Sam asks as a puzzled look crosses his face.

"Dr. Adring?" one asks.

"Yes... (He pauses)... What can I do for you?"

"Dr. Sam Adring?" the same one asks.

"Yes. What can I do for you?" sounding a little bit irritated.

"We need you to come with us. We can tell you no more. You will be briefed on everything you need to know… once we get to the labs", the other one says.

"Okay. Hold on a minute. I need to get a few things", as he turns around and grabs a coat and his briefcase.

Turning around he picks up the phone and says, "John. I have to go. I will call you as soon as I can. Good bye", as he hears John say good bye then he hangs the phone up.

Going to the bedroom he kisses Velma on the cheek and leaves her a note that he left with the 2 guys. Getting into their car as they open the door for him, he fidgets around until they get to the place where they are going. Pulling in through a security gate they find an empty slot and pull in. Escorting him through numerous checkpoints they arrive at a lab door. Upon entering he sees there are 5 other people here… in lab coats. Not recognizing anyone, he takes his jacket off. As soon as he has his coat off, a young gentleman comes over and gives him a lab coat in exchange for his overcoat. Trading and putting the lab coat on he goes over and starts asking the same questions he was been being asked. Finding that the shuttle caused the green glow, they tell him that it is not from the toxins that were aboard either.

"We can't explain it", one guy says, as he paces back and forth.

Walking over to a table with microscopes on it, he sees a fairly older gentleman looking at something through one. Going over to him, he asks, "So, what is your theory?"

"I don't have theories", he says, in a matter of fact tone.

"Fine", he says, as he walks away and starts looking at all their research.

As he looks around he wonders what he can do here, that he can't do at his place. Just then a guy in a gray suit walks in and says, "Ladies and gentleman. We have brought you here in the hopes you can tell us what this green glow is...and what caused it.... And... If the shuttle blowing up had anything to do with it... Now... if you will all follow me we are going to go aboard a ship and go out to the green glow area. From there is where you come in. You will be told everything you need to know once we are aboard the ship", as he waves for everyone to follow him.

Walking to the ship, they all get aboard and are told they can go anywhere on the ship they want. Nothing is off limits. Please.... Feel free to go on deck and see the green glow, first hand. Once everyone is aboard the ship starts moving. As the ship heads out to sea and towards the mysterious green emanation spilling from beneath the waters Sam goes up on deck and observes the ocean. Just then he sees something shoot out of the water and fly over his head. Oh shit.... He thinks to himself as he runs to the room where all the other doctors are milling about and tells them what he saw.

JANUARY 2, 2013
CHAPTER 4

As the alarm clock goes off Nick jumps out of bed and turns it off. Going into the kitchen he gets a pot of coffee brewing then he goes into the bathroom and takes a shower. By the time he gets done with his shower, the coffee is done. Drying off, he walks into the kitchen and picks up the hot coffeepot as he pours himself a cup of coffee. Getting another cup down he pours Amy a cup and takes them both into the bedroom, where he sets them down on the nightstand. Bending down, he kisses her cheek and gently shakes her. "Amy.... Amy... It's time to get up", he says, as he starts to laugh.

Turning over and mumbling something incoherent, she bunches the blanket up and snuggles with it. Shaking her a little more, he starts licking her face. She smacks his face as she reaches up to wipe her cheek. Moving his head he says in a more stern voice, "Amy. It's time to get up sleepyhead".

Opening her eyes a little at a time she rises up on one elbow, and says as she smiles. "Good morning babe".

"Good morning sweetie. Sleep well?" he asks as a smile plays on his lips.

"Yes.... Thank you. Oh, and thanks for the coffee", she says as she sees a cup of steaming hot coffee on the nightstand. Sitting up, she takes her cup and sips it.

"Anytime, babe", he says.

Looking at the clock she sees it is 5:30. Getting up she says, "Hey. You need to take me home so I can get ready for work. I have to be there in an hour".

"Yeah. I'm working on it. Let me get dressed and then we'll go... Okay?" as he looks for some clothes to wear.

"Okay", she replies smiling.

Finding some pants and a shirt, he turns around so his back is to her and starts getting dressed. After he is done they go out to the truck and he helps her in before getting in himself. Taking her home he goes back to his house and goes inside. Entering the office he checks his machine for messages. Writing down all the calls he turns the recorder to rewind and resets the machine. Looking at the addresses on the paper he sneers, as he sees that Frank called and said his a/c wasn't working. That figures. Grabbing his briefcase, he goes out front and sees Bill Gorbing, his assistant, waiting for him. "Good morning there Bill. Ready to get to work?" as he opens his door and puts his things inside.

As Nick unlocks the other door Bill gets in and says, "Mornin' to you to, bossman", as he laughs.

"Bossman my ass", Nick says laughing with him.

"Oh. Do you remember that job we did out in the middle of nowhere?" Nick asks.

"Yeah. That was a messed up job. Wait a minute… Don't tell me. He called and needs us to look at it", he says as he gets a down look on his face.

"That's the one. He said the fan isn't working. I think he's crazy. That was a brand new unit we put in his place", Nick says as he thinks about it.

Talking and laughing on the way, they finally get to Frank's house and go up the drive. Seeing no other cars in the drive Nick assumes everyone is gone. Stopping the truck he gets out and tells Bill to grab the gauges, Freon-22, a rag and a pair of pliers, as he grabs his ohmmeter. Walking around back Nick goes over to the unit and remembers he needs a drill. Walking back to the truck he runs into Bill, who happens to have the drill with him. Taking the drill he walks over and opens the unit up. Depressing the contactor the fan starts up. Just then they hear something rustling out in the woods. Looking towards the woods, which are only 25 feet away, they look and see if they can see anything.

Not hearing anything else, Nick continues his inspection of the unit and is just about to turn it on, when he hears the noise again. "Bill.... Did you hear that?" Nick whispers with a scared tone to his voice.

"Yeah. What do you think it is? An alligator?" Bill whispers back.

"I don't know. Whatever it is, it's starting to get me worried", he replies.

Waiting for a few minutes and looking at the woods, Nick decides it must be a small animal. Turning back to the unit with his back to the woods, he sends Bill to the truck for a new contactor. Turning the power off, Nick starts removing the old contactor a shadow blocks his light. "Hey Bill. Move it!" Nick says as he turns around and sees this huge thing. It's at least 7 feet tall… and a godawful face on each side of its head, (he sees this, as the creature turns its head), coming toward him not more than ten feet away. "BILL", Nick yells as he backs up and trips over the Freon.

Just then Bill comes running around the corner. As he sees the thing he stops dead in his tracks. As they look at the thing and as Nick is trying to get away, the thing starts shaking and splits into two. One goes after Nick and the other goes after Bill. Panicking Nick grabs the gauges that are hooked up to the Freon. Pointing the hose at the thing he opens the valve all the way, and sprays the thing with a burst of instant freeze. As the thing writhes in agony and pain, (or so it seems to Nick because the thing is making a high-pitched squeal that starts hurting his ears), he sprays the thing with as much of the Freon as he can.

Out front Bill is running for his life as the thing chases him. He runs through some trees and tries losing the thing as he figures 2 people working together are better than one and he runs around the other side of the house and sees Nick, spraying the one in back with the Freon. Running up behind him Nick turns around as he hears something coming up and sprays Bill with the Freon. Spraying him for only a couple of seconds Nick says, "Bill. Watch it. Behind you", as he goes around Bill and starts spraying the other thing with the Freon.

Squealing louder than the last one it falls down just as the tank runs dry. Walking over to it Nick kicks it and backs away quickly, staring at it as he hears something and turns around and sees the other one still moving toward him, with all four hands reaching for him. Just then Bill comes around the corner with a fresh bottle of Freon and sprays the thing until it falls. "What the hell are those.... Those... things, Bill asks as he looks around to make sure there are no more coming.

"I haven't got the slightest clue. Whatever they are we need to tell someone", Nick says.

Walking to the truck Nick dials 911 on his cell phone and relates what just happened, and where, and that they will need to bring either a coroner or an ambulance or just a big Damn truck", Nick says, as he trembles ever so slightly.

"Sir. We have some vehicles on their way", the operator says in a nasally voice.

"Okay. Thanks", Nick says as he heaves a sigh of relief.

Walking back around the house he tells Bill to go out front and wait for the cops and ambulance.

Bring them back here when they arrive Nick tells him as he turns to leave.

Walking out front Bill waits for the cops. Once they arrive he shows them out back. Looking at the thing's laying on the ground, the cops ask Nick questions like, "What is it? Where did it come from?"

"How the hell am I supposed to know? I just froze the bastards. Try sneaking up on me again you son of a bitches", as he kicks the closest one.

"Hey, hey, hey", one cop says, "I think you killed it".

"Yeah.... I hope I did. The bastards tried sneaking up on me", he says shaking slightly, with a slight tremble to his voice.

As he pulls his radio out one cop walks a short distance away and starts talking. Nick sees him shaking his head. Every once in awhile, the cop looks at them and shakes his head. Not liking what he is seeing Nick walks over to Bill and says in a whisper that only Bill can hear, "Hey Bill, something's fishy here. I think they're going to take us in and try to ask us questions for awhile. I myself... don't really want to go answer any questions... if you know what I mean?" as he keeps an eye on the cops.

"So, what do you think we should do?" Bill asks.

"I say... we run out front and jump into my truck and haul ass. Once we get away from the cops we can figure out what to do then", Nick suggests.

Shaking his head up and down and laughing, Bill says, "Okay. Just say the word".

"Okay. When I say, Hell Bill, be prepared to run like hell and jump in the truck", Nick says as he lays the plan out.

Noticing the cop still over talking on his radio, Nick says out loud, "Hell Bill", as he turns and runs out to the front.

As he runs out front he opens his door and starts the truck up just as Bill jumps in. Putting the gear into reverse Nick spins his wheels and backs out of the drive. As the tires hit the pavement, they squeal. Putting the gear in drive, Nick floors the gas pedal and squeals his tires as he takes off. Running after him the cop on the radio jumps into his cruiser and takes off in pursuit. Backing out of the drive the cop turns on his lights and siren as he jams his gear into drive and squeals his tires.

Looking in his rearview mirror, Nick doesn't see any cops coming yet, and turns right onto a four by track. Driving down the track they soon come to a dead end. "Damn", Nick mutters.

"Hey. You can go over there… and it will take you up to a farm… a short ways up the road from that job we were just at", Bill says as he points in the direction he is talking about.

"Okay. Let's do it", as he turns the wheel and drives to where Bill was pointing.

Driving the way as Bill tells him where to go they are soon back on pavement. Heading away from the scene Nick goes the back way to his house. As they approach the house they can see cop cars all over the place. Turning onto a side road just before his house, Nick drives down it and pulls in behind his barn and shuts the truck off. Getting out and leaving the door open, Nick looks around the corner and sees cops all over inside and outside of his house. Going back to the truck, Nick tells Bill to get out and quietly shut your door. As they shut the doors Bill follows Nick to a small shack out back.

Taking his keys out of his pocket Nick unlocks the door and opens it slowly so as to avoid any unwanted noise. Looking inside Bill sees a nice, brand new hot rod sitting there. It is glossy black with gold metal flake. Whistling lightly, Bill says. "Nice set of wheels, Bossman", as he starts to laugh slightly.

"Thanks. I keep it out here for just such situations like this", he replies.

Getting in Nick starts up the car and pulls it out. Closing the doors as Nick pulls out; he puts the lock back on. Walking to the car Bill gets in and Nick says, "Where do you want to go Bill?"

"I don't have anywhere I need to go. My only vehicle is out front of your house", he says as he shrugs his shoulders.

"Well… if you don't mind going with me, I think we might be better off. Like they say… two heads are better than one", Nick says and starts laughing.

Pulling onto Old Tampa Highway Nick drives west and pulls into the drive where Amy works. As he pulls up to the building Nick notices only one car in the whole lot. It belongs to Amy. Pulling up next to her car Nick and Bill get out and go in. Entering the building they feel a slight chill. Rubbing his arms Nick calls out, "Amy. You here?"

Not getting a response Nick walks behind the desk and enters the labs. Looking around he sees the bones. Going over with Bill following him he says, "These look like our friend we killed".

"Yeah. But what are they doing here?" Bill asks.

"They were sent here from a mining company yesterday", Amy says as she leans against the doorframe.

Smiling at her Nick says, "You don't look to good babe. Why don't you go home and get some rest? Oh… by the way. We were out doing a service call at Frank's place and we were attacked by one of these... Things..." he says, as he points at the bones.

"What do you mean by one of these... Things?" she asks.

"I mean, we were attacked by one of these... Things it was at least 7 feet tall. It tried to sneak up on Bill and me. But I froze the bastards", Nick says as he smiles.

"I was thinking about going home. I called up Velma, my boss's wife, and she said she would not be in today because she isn't feeling very well either".

"Well… you should. Oh and by the way, if the cops come looking for me, you never saw me today except this morning, okay?" he asks.

"Okay. What did you do this time?" she asks, as she smiles at him.

"We took off from the job while they were there still. I think they were going to take us in and ask us questions forever. I myself, will not be a party to that", Nick replies as he smiles back.

Going over to her he lets her lean against his shoulder. Feeling her forehead he says, "My god babe. You're burning up. Come on. Let's get you home", he says as he takes her out to his car and helps her in.

"Bill. Sit tight. I will be back in a few", Nick says as he backs out and takes Amy home.

"Okay", Bill says as Nick backs out and waves.

As he pulls out Nick looks in his rearview mirror and sees Bill waving. Feeling her head, her skin feels like it is on fire. Thinking better of it he decides to take her to the hospital. Driving her into town he goes to the local hospital. Pulling into the emergency room entrance, he pulls up outside the emergency doors and puts the car in park. Leaving the car running he carries her inside and says, "Someone. Help. Get me a gurney", as he looks around trying to find somewhere to put her.

"What's wrong with her?" a young Doctor asks, as he comes over.

"I don't know. I just know she is on fire. Here, feel her forehead", Nick says.

"Hmmm", the doctor hums, as he feels her forehead, then he yanks his hand away. "Damn. She is on fire. Nurse. Get me an ICU room right away. This girl needs to get into a tub of ice stat", he yells out as nurse's start running around getting him the things he needed.

"Do you think she will be all right? I can't lose her doc", Nick says as tears come to his eyes, while rolling her down the hall and into the elevator.

"I don't know until I run some tests. I am not going to lie to you though. I don't think she'll make it", he says as he looks down at the floor.

"Noooooooooo", Nick says as he bangs his fists on the elevator walls.

"Calm down now. I know you are upset, but rest assured I'll do everything I can to save her. I give you my word", the doctor says as he looks at his back.

Turning around Nick looks into the doctor's eyes and sees he is telling the truth. "Thanks doc. I have faith in you. Just take good care of her. And if you need any cash for any tests, or any special care, just call me at this number", as he takes out a business card and writes his cell phone number on the back. "Anytime… day or night. Here", as he hands the doctor his card.

"I don't see we will need that at this time. Just go home right now and when I find something out, I will call and let you know. Now go home and get some rest", the doctor says as he pats Nick on the back and rolls the gurney into the hallway and down the corridor.

Turning to the left at the end Nick looks on until she is gone. Tears start streaming down his face as he takes the elevator down. Getting off the elevator he walks out to his car and leaves. Driving around aimlessly, he realizes Bill is still waiting for him back at Amy's work. Heading toward her work he drives by his house. As he drives by he sees a cop in the lane by his house, just waiting for him to come home. As he keeps driving he turns onto the road that her work is on. Pulling into the parking lot, Nick beeps his horn.

Coming out of the building Bill starts in on him, "Where the hell ya been man? I been here, waitin' an hour and a half!"

"Hey Bill. I was driving her home and I reached over and felt her forehead. My god Bill... it was almost as hot as touching a stove burner. So I took her to the hospital. Hey I'm sorry about that but I have to take care of her. Can you understand man?" Nick says, as he looks at Bill and lets him see the pain in his eyes.

"Hey I'm sorry man. I didn't know. Jeez... I hope she's all right man. I'm sorry for yelling at you. Now I feel like such an asshole", he says as he apologizes.

"Hey... that's all right man. I just have to do what I feel is right. Know what I mean?" he asks as he winks at Bill and smiles.

"Yeah", Bill replies as he smiles back.

"So... where do we go now Bill?" Nick asks.

"I'm not sure. We obliviously can't go back to your place... or mine either" he states as he shrugs his shoulders. "What do you think we ought to do?" he asks back.

"I was thinking about going to the beach", he says as he smiles a crazy smile.

"What the hell are you wantin' to go to the beach for? Man.... You must be crazy", he replies as he looks at Nick, and they both start laughing.

After getting control of his laughing Nick says to Bill, "No. I want to go check out this green glow I seen last night coming from over where the shuttle blew up".

"No shit", Bill says.

"No shit man. I recorded the shuttle blowing up and then that night, I went out and looked and saw a green glow coming from the east. So I figure we should go see it if you are game that is Bill?" Nick asks as he raises one eyebrow and starts laughing.

"What the hell. I don't have much else to do", he replies.

Heading to eastbound 192 Nick stops one time for gas and drinks. When they get going they laugh and crack jokes as they head to the beach.

# CHAPTER 5

As the ship arrived at the green glow the ship starts to slow up and then it comes to a complete stop. As all the scientists are looking over the edge of the ship at the green glow, Sam sees the man whom he had talked with in the room. Going over to him Sam says, "Excuse me".

"Yes. What can I do for you Dr.?" he asks questioningly.

"I need to get some water samples and then I will want to send down sound buoys. I need equipment... a few men to take my orders so we can see what we are dealing with", Sam says as if has given orders all his life.

"You got it. How many men do you need?"

"About four".

"Okay. Nicky! You and Jimmy... and let's see... Stephen... And Lance. Go with Dr. errrr... What was your name again, Dr.?

"Dr. Sam Adring", he replies.

"Go with Dr. Adring and get him anything he needs and help in any way you can, and of course within reason. Does that help Dr. Adring?" the man asks.

"Yes. Thank you sir. I will send you any results I find ASAP. And again thanks", Sam says as he takes the guys and walks to the edge of the boat.

He points over the boat and talks to the guys, explaining to them what he needs and why he needs it. Nodding their heads in agreement they scatter and go in different directions. Within fifteen minutes they are back with everything he asked for. Smiling he then explains that he wants them to drop down over the edge… (As they nod)… and get some water samples… from various depths. Lance volunteers and rigs up a tether as Jimmy is cranking up the engine for the hoist. As the motor rumbles to life, they all feel the vibration. Looking at each other they all smile together.

Attaching a close clasp hook to the body harness Lance is wearing, Sam hands him everything he needs. Hoisting him up Jimmy extends the boom and starts rotating the boom slowly. Once Lance is hanging over the water something comes up and takes Lance in one gulp. Everyone jumps back, startled… and frightened. As it sinks in almost everyone runs like scared rabbits. Looking over the edge Sam looks down as the creature submerges in the water. "WHAT THE HELL WAS THAT… DR", Jimmy asks looking as terrified as the Dr. is feeling.

"I have no idea Jimmy. Your guess is as good as mine", Sam says to Jimmy as the scientist in him starts coming out again.

Going over to the hoist Sam rotates the boom and swings it onboard. As he gets it over the edge he lowers the boom and stops it four feet above the deck. Turning the engine off he goes over and starts examining the wire cable, without touching it. Looking at it he notices it looks like it was burned off. "That's odd", Sam says not realizing he was saying it out loud.

"What's that... Dr.", Jimmy asks.

"Huh", Sam says as he turns around and looks at Jimmy.

"You said, that's odd, and I asked you what?" Jimmy replies getting his color back.

"Oh. The wire cable looks like it was burned off. But what I can't figure is it would take a tremendous amount of energy... somehow bottled up and let loose at one time. It would have to be thousands of amps... bottled up. I mean we are talking a massive amount of energy and we just don't have the technology for that", he tells Jimmy.

"And this means... what, Dr.?" Jimmy asks.

"It means that we are most likely dealing with advanced alien life-forms. Something from outer space is all that I can think of. Unless... maybe you have a suggestion... Jimmy?" he asks.

"Sounds better than what I was thinking it could be", he said as he smiled.

"And what could that be Jimmy?" Sam asks.

"I was thinking… that maybe… you know… it was some kind of sea creature that lives in the sea", he says as he smiles over at Sam.

"HA… HA… HA… Sam laughs. "Don't get me wrong Jimmy but I don't think we have any sea monsters on our planet, or we would have seen them by now", he says as his laughing subsides.

Just then the water starts bubbling up all around the boat. It starts lifting and yawing back and forth violently as everyone on board falls down as the boat pitches. Sam hears screams coming from somewhere below as he loses and then regains consciousness. Touching his head he feels a big lump. That must be where I hit my head as I fell down…. He thinks to himself. The ship is now sitting on top of something huge. Sam sees they are rising into the air. Making his way over to Jimmy as the ship rises up, he grabs him and checks for a pulse. Feeling a light one he tries to wake him up. "JIMMY………. WAKE UP……… DAMMIT JIMMY", Sam screams at him.

Opening his eyes he looks at Sam and says, "I heard you. You don't have to yell", as the ship starts sliding off the huge thing.

"Come on Jimmy. We need to get on a life raft and get the hell out of hear", Sam says with the utmost urgency in his voice.

Holding onto the railing they both stand up and look for the nearest life raft. Looking both ways Jimmy looks across the deck and says, "Hey… Over their… on the other side", as he points across the deck.

Looking over Sam says, "We will have to be careful in case the ship starts shifting again", he says.

"Ready?" Sam asks.

"As ready as I'll ever be", Jimmy replies back.

"Then let's go", Sam says as they both let go of the rail and run across the deck to the boat.

Looking at it Sam is satisfied with the condition of it. "Jimmy. We need to lower it as far as we can and then get into it and hit the emergency release", Sam tells him.

Nodding his head he motions for the Dr. to get in. "I will lower it. Once I go as far as I can I will climb down the cable and into the boat. Now go. Hurry", Jimmy says as he goes over to the controls and starts the motor and gets it ready to lower the boat into the water.

Climbing in the boat the doctor takes the tarp off the boat and climbs in as the boat starts to lower much too slow for Jimmy's taste. Hurry up.... He thinks to himself. Damn slow ass motors they have these days. Noticing something hanging under the controls he finds a roll of tape hanging underneath the control box. Picking it up he tapes the control lever to lower the boat. As the boat continues to lower Jimmy runs over to the side and grabs hold of the cable. Once he is hanging by the cable he shimmies down it. About halfway down the ship starts sliding again as the cable starts swaying back and forth as it knocks Jimmy against the hull of the ship. Just then the boat stops and the cable quit lowering at the same time and jars Jimmy from the rope. Looking down as he falls he sees nothing but empty space to the ocean. Praying quietly to himself he comes to an abrupt halt as he lands in the bottom of the boat. As he hit the bottom of the boat the breath was knocked out of him.

The Dr. goes over to him and does something to him and he catches his breath. Breathing in and out he heaves from having the breath knocked out of him. Catching his breath he tells the Dr. to get ready to hit the release. Nodding his head the doctor belts himself into a seat and asks, "Ready".

Closing his eyes and nodding his head up and down Sam hits the release button. As he pushes the button the boat falls and instantly Sam feels his stomach somewhere up above him and his eyes seem to bulge out as the boat falls. Looking over at Jimmy Sam sees him braced across the bottom of the boat. As the boat hits the water below they are jarred as if someone had a fist the size of your body and just hauled off and hit you, but good. As they lie there the boat starts drifting under the thing. Opening his eyes Sam sees they are directly underneath the ship. "Oh shit", he says.

Going to the controls he starts the motor up and revs it up to full throttle as they start moving away from the thing. When they are about a hundred and fifty feet away the ship falls down and plunges into the ocean. As it lands sideways in the water it creates a huge wave that is heading towards them. Looking back as he tries to guide the boat away from the wave, the boat starts turning around as the wave approaches. Trying desperately to correct it the wave hits and turns the boat around in circles as it rocks. Feeling like he is going to fall out of the boat it stops turning after a few minutes.

As the water calms down some Sam goes over to the controls and heads the boat in what he thinks… is the shore.

## CHAPTER 6

As they get to the beach, they head south following the green glow. As they head south, Nick looks up and sees two things flying fast and low into the woods off to the right of him. Looking for a road he happens to see one and slams on the brakes. "Hey! What are you doing man?" Bill asks.

"I saw something fly in here. I want to see what it was", Nick says as he drives into the woods.

As they get a couple of miles into the woods they see a strange, light green glow, emanating from the woods. Turning his lights off Nick pulls a little closer and then cuts the engine. Getting out of the car Bill says, "Hey. Are you crazy cracker? You won't get me going towards no glowing shit!" he states.

"SHHHHHhhhh… "Nick says, as he looks at Bill and puts his finger to his lips.

Creeping toward the green glow Nick has a baseball bat in his right hand. The one he keeps behind his seat just for these kinds of occasions and others. As he gets closer he sees three shapes moving around. Creeping closer he gets to within fifteen feet of them, before he stops and stares. My god... He thinks.... What the hell are they? Wanting to get a better look Nick creeps closer yet. Just as he gets to within ten feet of them, he steps down and a branch cracks. Looking at the creatures he sees them stop and look in his direction. Staying as still as he can he keeps an eye on the things.

Making strange noises and pointing with all four hands, one of the creatures starts coming toward him. "SHIT", Nick yells as he gets up and runs back to the car. Looking behind him as he runs he hits his head on a branch and falls down. "DAMN", he curses.

Getting up he regains his footing and keeps on running. As he gets close he yells out, "BILL START THE CAR NOW", as he runs around a tree and sees the car come into view.

Starting the engine Bill sees Nick running toward the car. Putting one foot on the brake Bill puts the gearshift into reverse. As Nick jumps in and closes the door, he says, "Hang on to your ass... cause we are in trouble", as he guns the engine and starts driving backward.

Looking at the dash, Nick reaches over and hits his headlights. As he is driving backwards he sees a good spot to turn around coming up. He gets himself ready for the turn around as he slams on the brakes and cuts the wheel hard left. Gunning the gas, the car spins around. As the car spins and is almost to the point Nick wants it, he turns the wheel to the right until the wheels are straight and lets off the brake. The car lurches forward and jerks him hard. As Nick hits his head against the steering wheel Bill is rubbing his head and putting his seatbelt on as he says, "You are one crazy freaking cracker man".

"If you want to live in this world you have to be crazy yourself", Nick says as he looks at Bill and smiles crazily.

"Man, you are one crazy freakin' dude", Bill states as he starts laughing knowing Nick is an all right guy.

Bursting out into laughter Nick looks up and sees the thing that he saw earlier and followed, fly over the top of them and disappear over the trees. "I don't like that", Nick says.

"Me either", Bill says. "You don't think they are going to fly ahead and ambush us… do you?"

"I don't know man. I sure hope the hell not", Nick says as he continues driving.

As they are driving Nick sees something in the way about a hundred feet ahead. Slowing down a little he sees it is one of those things. "Bill. Do you see what I see?" he asks as he pushes the accelerator to the floor.

"Yeah. Run them son of a bitches down, man", he says, as he starts getting nervous.

As they get right on top of it Nick looks at the speedometer and sees he is doing forty-five. This will surely kill them bastards... He thinks. As he hits the thing the car comes to an abrupt stop. On impact, Nick and Bill are thrown against the dash. Shaking his head and trying to get his wits about him, Nick looks out the window and sees the thing reaching for the door. Twisting the key Nick doesn't get anything. Looking around he finally realizes the car is still in drive. Putting the lever in neutral, Nick tries again. The thing reaches up and pulls the door off as the engine roars to life with a hell of a rattling in the front. Shoving the lever into drive, Nick floors the pedal and speeds off down the path.

Finally seeing the pavement about fifty feet ahead he pulls out onto it without slowing down. Heading south he tries to wake Bill up as he shakes him. "Bill… Hey Bill", he says as he shakes him. "WAKE THE HELL UP, DAMMIT", he yells.

Finally, Bill starts moving. Opening his eyes he asks, "What the hell happened", as he sits up.

"They almost got us. Damn things were right there. Look at my freaking door. The bastard tore the sons of a bitch right the hell off. They are some tough creatures", Nick says as he notices a wobble in the steering wheel.

Just then the two craft fly by overhead and disappear to the east into the green glow. "Screw the hell out of me", Nick says as he watches them fly off. "I bet them bastards are coming from the green glow", he states as he notices the wobble getting worse.

Seeing his hands shaking from the car Bill asks, "What's wrong with the car?"

"It was the bastard we hit. He didn't budge when we hit him. We did", Nick says.

"Well let's hope we can make it to the next gas station so we can get it fixed", Bill says.

Laughing as Bill says that the front right tire blows out and grabs the car and tries to force them off the road. Grabbing the wheel with everything he can he fights it until he can get it to slow down and pull over. Stopping the car and cutting the engine off Nick kicks the tire and yells, "YOU GOD DAMN MOTHER FREAKIN PIECE OF SHIT. BUILT TOUGH MY ASS", as Bill starts laughing at Nick going off.

"What the hell are you laughing at?" he says as he catches a glimpse of himself in the mirror and starts laughing with him.

"I guess you see what I'm laughing at... huh?" Bill says as he starts cracking up again.

As they get control of themselves they get Bill goes to the trunk and Nick looks at the blown tire. Sauntering around for a last look at the damage, he walks around the car. As he gets to the front and sees the damage the thing caused, he whistles. Coming from the back of the car Bill is carrying the jack and four-way lug wrench. Handing them to Nick he looks at the front end and whistles himself. "And you are trying to tell me... that one of those things did this?" Bill asks.

"Hell yeah. I was doing forty-five and it did not budge an inch. It is the god damnedest thing I ever saw", Nick says as he loosens the lugs.

Finally getting the tire changed they put away the jack, blown tire and the lug wrench and then get in. Nick gets in and tries to start the car. As the engine grinds slowly at first, it kicks over and catches. As it roars to life, he puts it in drive and keeps heading south. As they drive down the road they see something ahead. Slowing down a little Nick clicks on the high beams and only the left one works. Pulling to the right a little they see it is one of those things, standing in the road. "Holy shit", Nick says as he sees five of them standing across the road.

"Go around them", Bill says.

Veering the car to the left they drive up the side and before he has time to see anything, they run right into the ocean as the car stalls in the knee-deep surf. Looking back he doesn't see them coming yet. Let's get the eff out of here Bill", Nick says as he gets out of the car.

Bill gets out as Nick does and they wade to shore and run off down the beach. Seeing a house ahead, they run toward it. As they are running, Nick looks back over his shoulder and sees the things coming after them. Running even faster now he passes Bill up. As Nick passes him up Bill looks over his shoulder and sees them coming and knows why Nick sped up. Running like a bat out of hell, he catches up with Nick and they finally get to the house. Banging on the door Nick yells out, "HELLO. ANYBODY HOME?"

Noticing a light come on Nick mumbles to himself, "Come on, come on", as he wiggles his legs. As the front light comes on they hear the person behind the door unlocking it. As the door starts to open Nick and Bill burst in. Knocking the guy over Nick turns around and shuts and locks the door. "Sorry about that mister. But you have to understand something first. Do you have any guns", he asks as he sounds like he is ranting and raving.

Shaking his head the guy says, "Y-Yeah u-upstairs", as he points to the stairs.

Running up the stairs Bill stays and explains the situation to the guy. Shaking his head the guy says, "You are both a couple of lunatics".

"WHERE ARE THE BULLETS AT?" Nick can be heard asking as his voice comes down the stairs.

"Where the bullets at", Bill asks as one of the things, pulls the door off its hinges and throws it to the side.

Backing up toward the stairs Bill yells out, "NICK. HURRY UP... THEY'RE HERE!

"WHERE THE HELL, ARE THE BULLETS?" Nick yells out again.

"I-In t-t-the d-d-d-dresser d-drawer", the man stutters.

"IN THE DRESSER DRAWER", Bill yells to Nick as he starts climbing up the stairs as the creature stops and starts shaking. As it's shaking stops it splits into 2 creatures.

Bill runs up the stairs and grabs anything within his grasp and throws it at the creatures. Throwing a picture at the creature the glass breaks and cuts one of its eyes off. Squealing... In oblivious pain... It starts turning around and smashing things. "WHERE YOU AT, NICK?" Bill yells as he gets upstairs.

"In here", Nick says.

Going in the direction his voice came from Bill looks back and sees one of the creatures tearing the man in half, with its bare hands.... Or whatever they are called.... Bill thinks to himself. Finding the bullets Nick loads up a 12 gauge double barrel shotgun. Handing a 30-30 to Bill, he hands him the bullets and steps out into the hallway. As he steps out, he sees the outline of one of those things, coming up the stairs. Standing around the corner, he gathers his guts up and steps out as he pulls both triggers at the same time. As the bullets bounce off the thing, Nick steps back around the corner and into the bedroom. "Bill", he says.

"Yeah, Nick?" Bill asks.

"We need to get the eff out of here. They are upstairs and bullets don't hurt them at all. Quick, open the window", Nick says with authority in his voice.

Used to taking orders from Nick, Bill goes to the window and tries to open it, but it won't budge. "Damn things painted shut", Bill says with a note of worry in his voice.

"Break the damn thing then", Nick says as he pushes the bed in front of the door.

Grabbing a chair, Bill throws it through the window as he hears a crash coming from behind him. Looking back he says, "To hell with this", as he jumps out the window and lands in a pile of sand.

Seeing the bed did no good Nick runs to the window and looks back as the creature throws the bed aside, like a bag of potatoes. Nodding his head, he jumps out the window as he says, "Coming down".

As he lands in the pile of sand that Bill did, Bill comes over and helps him up and says, "There are three more out front and six more ships...

landing out back. What the hell are we going to do now?" Bill asks Nick.

"Shhhhhhhh", Nick says, as he puts his finger to his lips. "Let's sneak over to them weeds and see if we can crawl up to the road, without them seeing us".

Shrugging his shoulders Bill says, "I don't care. Let's just get the hell out of here".

As they creep through the weeds, they get to the road. As they look in both directions, they don't see any of those things anywhere nearby. Getting up they both run down the road, near the trees, trying to keep as inconspicuous as possible. As they run down the road, they see three of their crafts fly by overhead and disappear from view.

# CHAPTER 7

As the big ship lifts into the air, other smaller crafts swarm out of the Triangle and head out, in all directions. As they swarm across the planet, they take out all the air bases as if they knew where all the air bases were. Even the ones that are not known. Not having a chance to retaliate, some small groups get together and start fighting back. As the people learn more, they start taking some of their pod like ships.

Meanwhile, aboard the big ship;

"Grseru ndhyr arenhok, (We have taken over all of their air bases commander)", one says to another.

"Good. Now we need to get rid of all the humans, except for five hundred thousand. We need to send them back to the other planet and see if they can breed new humans for slaves for us, (as he did what we would call a laugh I guess, as his voice roars out as if in triumph). Now go and give me a full report by tomorrow", the commander says.

"Yes sir", as the young soldier claps all four hands and stomps twice as he turns to leave.

"Krulgerin?" Knightwarp says.

Turning around, Krulgerin says, "Yes commander".

"What are the stats... on those small groups of humans... the ones that are giving us trouble?" he asks.

"Well sir. They are still on the loose. I have reports coming in that they have taken out some of our troops. They seem to know what hurts us. They are using special agents to kill our people... sir" Krulgerin says as he lowers his eyes.

"I want you to take care of this problem... immediately. We need to have the planet and all its resources by the third kieglor. We don't have time to waste. Now... get on it and be done by the time the Kiestoriel is here. If you fail me on this I will have you held fully responsible... for all the problems and make sure you are defratsitized. Now get this done and I want a report every Stroxtin", Knightwarp says.

"Yes sir, Commander Knightwarp", Krulgerin says as he bows and licks the floor, where Knightwarp's feet are.

"Go... and report back when you eliminate them", Knightwarp orders demandingly while he glowers at Krulgerin.

Turning around Krulgerin leaves and heads for the launch craft area. As he walks down the hall, Kinglesin greets him. He greets him back and continues on his way. As he gets near the launch craft area, he can hear a ruckus up ahead. Storming down the hall, he enters the labs and abruptly the conversation ends immediately.

"What is happening in here", Krulgerin demands.

"Nothing sir", Stiderion says.

"That is human, (bullshit), he says. I heard you down the hall and I demand an explanation, or you will all be defratsitized. And I will give your posts to your enemies", he says looking imposingly on them.

"We were just discussing, who would be a better commander than Knightwarp. We all agreed upon you... except Kinglesin... sir", Stiderion says.

"How dare you compare me to him. He is much better than I am and he has been in charge for five thousand Flixtorias. He will reign supreme over us until his death, which is another three hundred flixtorias. Now... get back to what you were doing and I don't want to hear any more about this", Krulgerin says, in his most intimidating voice.

They all stand up and clap their hands and stomp twice as they turn and leave.

Heading back to the launch area, Krulgerin walks in and sees his craft waiting for him. As he talks with the coordinator for takeoffs, he enters his craft and loads up in the launch area and shoots off.

As Knightwarp goes over to the command console, he looks and sees more casualties build up from various groups around the world. Beating on the console, he starts yelling out to everyone on the command deck, "I WANT THOSE HUMANS ANNIHILATED IMMEDIATELY", he demands.

"Yes sir, commander Knightwarp", Jinforin says. "I will personally see to it... that they are taken care of", as he claps his hands and stomps twice.

"Very well Jinforin. I have faith in you. I know you won't let me down. You never do and you always bring me what you say you will. Now go and find those humans and kill them all", Knightwarp says as he starts getting irate again.

Turning to go, Jinforin turns back and asks, "Commander?"

"Yes", Knightwarp says.

Can I take my new toy?" Jinforin asks.

"Yes. I would rather you did. Try it out and see how good it is. Very well then... go and report back as soon as you have the problem eliminated", Knightwarp orders.

"Yes sir, Commander Knightwarp", Jinforin says as he claps his hands and stomps twice again.

Turning to leave, Jinforin exits the command deck and goes to his special ship.

Knightwarp sits down and remembers the tales his creator told him, before he died. He had told him how he had led the raid on the planet and took it over.

Kimborin tells the tale of the switch.

It was the year of the Kingders. They were all our planet had left, after we used up all its resources. So we made a gateway... and when our people found this planet... we set up the doorway. Once we opened the doorway we took the creatures from our new planet and brought them here, to our old planet. Once they were out of our way we made all our weapons and advanced farther, (not realizing an intelligent creature would be created). Once we realized we had made a big mistake, it took us twenty thousand years to decide we needed our old planet back. Because of the lower gravity on our new planet we thought it would help us. Little did we know that when we finally figured out how to make doorways, using materials found only on our old planet we knew we had to have it back. That is when we decided to take it back, Knightwarp remembers.

## CHAPTER 8

**Meanwhile, back in the little town of Kissimmee:**

Lewis Smith is out in back of his house and sees Nick's truck sitting in the middle of the woods. Going over to it, he sees if the door is locked. Finding it unlocked, he opens it and checks the ignition. Not finding any keys in it, he checks around the truck, under the wheel wells to see if he keeps a spare somewhere. When he gets to the left front fender-well he feels around and feels a little box. Grabbing it he opens it and finds the key. Taking it out he gets in and starts the truck up. As he pulls it around to his house, he drives into the garage and shuts it off. Shutting the door he closes the garage door and locks it. Going back inside he turns the television on and lies down and goes to sleep. Waking up, he sees a news flash pop up.

Newscaster;

And, earlier today, the space shuttle Kennedy blew up and there still is no explanation as to why. And... As we.... Wait a minute. We just got this in. A huge ship of some kind has risen out of the Bermuda Triangle. It is about eighty miles long and four hundred miles wide. They say it is shaped like a couple of triangles with a ball on top. Wait a minute...They are saying a ship was caught on top of it...... It was a research vessel that had been checking out the green glow that appeared there after the shuttle blew up. We are getting reports...of strange... pod-like things... also coming out of the Bermuda Triangle. They say there are literally hundreds of them, swarming out of it. They say the pods are landing and things are coming out of them..... Huge things. My god... They're saying they are 7-8 feet tall and have four arms and three legs. They say their heads have faces on both sides and.... As snow fills the screen. Turning the channel Lewis gets nothing but snow on the screen.

"Holy shit", Lewis says as he turns the television off and goes over to the window and sees a couple of the pod like things fly by overhead. Packing a few things up he thinks he may need, he starts heading out the door as the phone rings. Going over to it he picks it up and says, "Hello".

"Lewis, is that you?" Nick asks as Lewis hears him breathing hard.

"Yeah. It's me bud. What's up, Nick? Hey, have you heard about these things... coming out of the Bermuda Triangle?" he asks as he sounds amazed and scared.

"Yeah… I heard about them. I ran into a couple of them this morning and have been going since. Lewis… I need a favor of you, if you can?" Nick asks as he starts catching his breath.

"Sure anything bud. What is it?" he asks.

"I need you to go and see if my truck is still out back of my place and bring it to me. What about it Lewis?" Nick asks as he sounds like he is begging.

"I already saw your truck earlier today, sitting out back and decided to see if you left your keys in it. I found them under the wheel well and parked it in my garage. You got it buddy. Where are you, anyway?"

"We are in a little town called Sebastian. How fast can you be here?" Nick asks him.

If I leave right now… I could be there in an hour or so. I have to pack my guns up", Lewis says.

Lewis hears him laughing as Nick replies, "Lewis. Guns don't faze them. I shot one at point blank range and it didn't do anything to him. But you can load up some Freon… from my garage. It's locked, but the key is hanging on a wire, under the step", Nick tells him. "And hurry man. I don't know how long we have until they find us… again".

"Okay buddy. I will be there as soon as possible. See you in a little while. And.... Take care", he says.

"All right buddy. Good-bye for now. See you in a little bit. And don't try to run them over either. I need my truck in one piece", Nick says.

"Okay. I know. See you soon buddy", Lewis says as he hangs the phone up and goes out to the garage and gets in Nick's truck. Starting it up he pulls out of the garage and drives over to Nick's place. Backing up to the door he finds the key and opens it up. Looking inside Lewis sees hundreds of bottles of Freon... Nick has stock piled. Grabbing a can at a time, he puts 12 into the bed of the truck. Sweating profusely he wipes sweat off his forehead as he gets into the truck and starts it up. Giving it a little gas, it leaps forward. "Whoooaaa", Lewis says to himself.

Turning the headlights on Ken pulls onto the road and heads to 192 eastbound. As he pulls out, he can swear he sees Amy... Nick's fiancée walking down the road and she was naked. He slows down and is going to offer her a ride, when he sees these grotesque things sticking out of her... all over and her eyes don't look right. Flooring the gas pedal, he hauls ass. On his way to 192 he sees 12 of the things the news described and 4 of the pods, flying by overhead. Avoiding all of them, he finally gets onto 192 and starts heading east. As he drives he is cautious of anything that looks suspicious. Avoiding the creatures Lewis makes it onto A1A southbound. As he drives south he sees the things they are talking about. As he swerves to avoid one another one appears out of nowhere. "DAMN", he says out loud.

Turning the wheel left, then right, he finally gets through them. Stepping on the accelerator he is soon doing 85 down A1A.He thinks to himself as he drives.... What the hell is happening here? I will not let them win... I will help and do whatever it takes to eradicate them from the face of our planet... As he drives he sees a glow up ahead, as if he were getting near a town. Slowing down a little, Lewis sees that the glow is not a town but a bunch of those pod things in the middle of the road. Looking for a way off the road, he spots a side road and veers off onto it.

Driving through the woods he finally gets to a little dirt road. As he drives down it he sees houses, off in the distance, with all the lights on and those things moving through them.... Probably killing them off as they go along...he thinks. As he drives he finally gets to the town where Nick is. Turning his headlights off, as the streetlights are good enough, he slows down and drives real slow. Opening the window he hears Nick... calling out to him, "Hey Lewis. Over here", as he waves.

Seeing Nick he pulls over to him and stops the truck. Getting out Lewis asks, "What the hell is happening here, Nick?"

"I don't know Lewis. I only know... that these bastards showed up after the shuttle blew up and the green glow came. Other than that I haven't got a clue", Nick says all pumped up with adrenaline.

"Okay... so what can I do?" Lewis asks.

Looking like they are on a commando mission Nick replies, "First things first. We need to get some more gas and find a store where we can get something to eat. I am starved. Aren't you?" he asks Bill.

"Damn right I am. I have been hungry but when you have something chasing you, it don't matter anymore", Bill replies as he smiles.

"Okay. Let's go. We need to stop these things, at all costs", Nick says as he climbs into the drivers' seat and starts up his truck.

After Lewis and Bill get in Nick puts the truck in drive and drives slowly around town. As they are driving he notices lights on everywhere. "What do you make of this? Why are all the lights on?" he asks.

"I haven't got a clue", Bill replies.

"It means... they have killed all the people. I saw some of them things at a house, and they had all the lights on and they were looking for something", Lewis says.

"Well... let's find a store and get the hell out of this town", Nick says still looking around.

"You have my vote there", Lewis and Bill say together, as they look at each other and start laughing.

# CHAPTER 9

After surviving the wave, they finally make it to shore. As Sam looks up he sees hundreds of those little pod-like things, flying around. Not realizing it the things have taken control of all the bases around the world. As they swarm out of the green glow, they are around the planet within minutes. Taking out all the air bases instantly. Once the creatures showed up the females started mutating too. Now the fate of this planet rests in the hands of a few survivors. Stepping out of the boat both Sam and Jimmy look around to see if there are any of those things coming. Satisfied that they are alone Jimmy says, "We need to find some weapons".

"No... we need to get to a laboratory so I can see if there is anything that will stop this. I have never seen anything like this. I mean... we knew there was a possibility of an alien attack, but one from the ocean. From our own world", Sam says as he looks disheveled and frazzled.

"Okay then. Let's get going before any of those things find us", Jimmy says as he starts heading up the beach.

Following after him they reach the road and look to see if there are any towns nearby. Not seeing anything they decide to walk north on the road. As they walk they look up and see those pod-like vehicles swarming overhead going to where… who knows. Shaking his head Sam says, "I want to know what these things want".

"Yeah me too. I also want to know where they came from as well", Jimmy says.

As they walk Jimmy looks off to the left and sees a house nestled back in the woods, with all the lights on. "Hey Dr.", he says as he points to the house.

"Let's go", Sam says.

Walking toward the house they see movement in the windows. As Sam is about to step up on the porch he looks up and sees a creature… the likes of which he has never seen before. Grabbing Jimmy's shirtsleeve he pulls him into the trees and motions for him to be quiet. Hiding behind a tree Sam explains why he did what he did. Nodding his head Jimmy listens intently. "Okay. Here is what we need to do. First, we need to get rid of these things. Then we need to get into the house and see if there are any supplies we can use", Jimmy whispers.

"Okay. How do you suggest we get rid of these things?" Sam asks Jimmy.

"Hmmmmmmmm".... He hums and then snaps his fingers...."I got it... I will make a diversion and you run in and find what you can", Jimmy says.

"What the hell kind of diversion are we talking about?" Sam asks.

"You will know it… when you hear it", Jimmy replies as he sneaks around to the back of the house.

As he gets to the back Jimmy sees a bunch of the creatures, standing over by one of those pod things. Just then they start getting into the pod like things and taking off. As the last creature comes out and gets into a pod, Jimmy runs up the stairs and comes face to face with one of the creatures. Stopping before he gets too close, Jimmy turns around and runs. As he leads the creature out the back Sam notices no movement inside and figures Jimmy has distracted them. Going up the stairs slowly Sam finally gets into the house. Finding some food and a gun, he puts the gun in his pocket.

Picking up the phone, Sam checks to see if there is a dial tone. Hearing none, he puts the phone back. Going upstairs he looks around and finds an antique sword hanging on a wall. Taking it down he almost drops it. Damn... He mutters to himself. Just then he hears something downstairs and he goes to the top of the stairs and looks down from around the corner. Seeing Jimmy he whispers, "Jimmy, up here".

"Looking up Jimmy smiles and goes up."Did you find anything useful?" Jimmy asks.

"I found a gun and a sword. Here", Sam says as he hands Jimmy the sword.

Taking the sword they go downstairs. Rummaging around in the kitchen, Jimmy finds some keys in a drawer. Taking them he leads

Sam outside. As they are going outside Jimmy notices a switch marked garage and flips it up, as lights come on from a building across the way. Looking out the back door he sees a building out in the woods, about 15 feet from the house. Leading the way to the building he goes inside. Once inside he looks around and sees one of those things sitting down next to one of those pod things. Putting his finger to his lips he motions for the Dr. to be quiet. Trying to sneak up on the thing it notices him and starts coming after him. As it follows Jimmy, Sam is hiding behind a couple of boxes that are stacked up by the door. As Jimmy leads the creature outside Sam climbs into the pod thing and looks around.

Noticing what looks like a radically different concept of apparatus he looks over the console and looks at everything more closely. Just then he hears something outside and looks for a place to hide. Finding a little nook he cowers down and waits. "Dr.", he hears someone whisper.

Getting up and going to the hatch he whispers, "Jimmy. In here", Sam says as he waves to him.

Seeing the Dr., Jimmy goes up the hatch and goes inside. Looking around he whistles lightly. "Damn. Can you make out what all these things are for?" he asks Sam.

"I don't know. I would have to experiment with it to see", Sam says as he starts pushing things and pulling things.

Seeing what looks similar to a chair Jimmy sits down and starts playing with button-like and knob-like things. As Jimmy pulls something the craft takes off, straight up. "Oh shit", Jimmy says as he sees the Dr. getting up, off the floor.

"What the hell did you do?" Sam asks Jimmy.

"All I did, was pull this here thing and it went up", he replies sheepishly s as the thing goes up, even farther.

"Okay. So we know what makes it go up and down. Now all we have to figure out is what makes it go forward and left and right. This shouldn't be too hard", Sam says.

Trying different things Jimmy finds one that takes the craft forward. Going forward they come to a stop when he lets go of the thing. "Damn", Jimmy says as he lets go of the thing.

"Well… Aren't we pretty good at this", Sam says as he begins smiling.

Smiling back Jimmy plays around a little more and finds what seems to be, some kind of substance… that pops out at him as he twists a knob-like thing. As he tries to jump out of the way, his foot hits something on the floor. Looking where his feet were he sees some pedal or what could pass for a pedal.... He thinks. Sitting back in the seat he pushes on one of the pedals and the thing turns right. "All right", Jimmy says as he tries to get the hang of the craft.

"So… I see you have the knack for flying things?" Sam states.

Just then a squealing sound can be heard. It is faint at first and then it picks up in pitch. As Jimmy covers his ears and moves, his foot gets lodged between 2 of the pedals and the craft starts spinning out of control. As the pod heads toward the ground, Jimmy tries to get his foot unstuck. Not being very successful, the craft crashes into the ground as it throws Jimmy and Sam to the floor. They crash land on the side of the road, in the ditch where there is some water puddling from the recent storms. Shaking his head as he gets up Jimmy's foot is unstuck. Yeah… that figures…. Jimmy thinks. Going to the Dr., Jimmy tries to revive him. Finally opening his eyes Sam asks, "What the hell happened?"

"Umm. My foot kind of got stuck… between two of the pedals. I guess I should be careful, huh?" he asks with a slight grin on his face.

"Yeah… maybe. Let's get out of here", Sam says as he rises to his feet.

Looking over Jimmy sees the hatch tore off. Looking out he sees it laying about 20 feet away. Jumping down as it is about 8 feet to the ground, the Dr. jumps after him. Just then a truck pulls up and almost mows them down.

## CHAPTER 10

As they see one of the pod-like things spinning out of control, they follow it to see where it is going. Seeing it crash on the side of the road they drive up to it. As Nick sees figures emerge from it he slams on the gas pedal and tries to run them down. Just as they get close he notices they are not those things. Swerving to avoid hitting them, he stops the truck and gets out. "Sorry", Nick says as they approach Sam and Jimmy as he raises his hands in the air to call a truce.

"That's all right", Sam says. "I would probably do the same thing".

"So… how did you guys get your hands on one of their craft's?" Nick asks.

"We kind of borrowed it", Jimmy replies, smiling slightly. "Kind of a……… Trade Secret you might say", as he looks over at Sam and they smile.

"So… what's with all the canisters in your truck?" Sam asks.

"Oh… those", Nick says pointing to them. "That's freon. I found out it hurts them or kills them or something. I know it stops them", Nick says.

Just then 3 of the pod-like crafts fly by overhead and turns as they start heading back. "Jump in and let's go", Nick says as he sees the crafts coming back.

As everyone gets into the truck, Nick starts it up and heads for the woods. Making it just barely in time as one of the craft lands and the hatch opens. 3 of those… things come out. They go over and look at the craft that Jimmy crashed. Looking around they happen to see the truck and point at it. "Oh shit", Nick says as he floors the accelerator.

As Sam looks back he sees the things… get into their crafts and coming after them. As they are going through the woods, Nick notices the sun starting to come up. "Damn", Nick says. "We have to find a place to hole up… until tonight".

"Why is that?" Sam asks.

"Because. In the daytime they will notice us more. I think we have a better chance of staying alive, if we can hide until dark", Nick says as Jimmy nods his head in agreement.

"Okay. I know where there is a lab about 5 miles away", Sam says. Just then one of the pod-like crafts comes crashing through the trees and lands in front of them. Slamming on the brakes Nick spins the wheel and avoids hitting the thing. Getting out of the truck Nick says, "Everyone, grab a bottle with a hose and get ready", as he grabs one and gets ready to spray the bastards.

As everyone grabs a canister, they move and spread out as they hide behind trees and rocks, while Nick stands in the open. As the creatures see Nick they start moving toward him. As they get to within 10 feet Nick opens the valve on the Freon and starts spraying the things. As the first one starts to freeze, it falls over and the other's coming for him. Just then everyone jumps out and starts spraying them, from all directions. As the last one falls to the ground Nick goes over to the pod-like thing and looks inside. As he looks he whistles lightly and says, "And you know how to fly this thing?" he asks as he looks at Jimmy.

"Sort of. But a high-pitched squeal started and when I covered my ears, I moved and my foot got stuck between 2 of the pedals and that's when it started going out of control", Jimmy explains.

Nodding his head Nick says, "Well... seeing as you know how to fly one you can teach all of us, so we can see about taking them out... with their own ships", as he smiles devilishly.

As Jimmy gives them a crash course they all try out on them, and soon they are flying them like pros. "Okay. We need to have these craft where the lab is at, so we can study them a little bit. Bill, you take one. Jimmy can take one and Lewis can go with you Jimmy and I will take one and let the Dr. take my truck. I will follow the Dr.", Nick says as he heads for one of the crafts. As they all go to their pods they all take off. As Sam pulls out and onto the road Jimmy and Bill go ahead and scout out the area ahead. As Nick plays with the controls a green energy like pulse comes out the front. "WOW", Nick says to himself.

Looking up Sam sees the energy pulse as well and says, "Damn".

As Sam looks back at the road he turns the wheel to avoid hitting 2 of the creatures. As Nick sees the creatures standing in the road he takes his craft down and starts firing those green pulses at them. As they impact on the ground near them, they explode in brilliant colors. Hitting both of them they blow up into tiny pieces. "YEAH", Nick yells as he gives himself a high-five.

"Damn if he ain't getting the hang of these things", Sam mumbles.

As Nick clears all the things out of Sam's way, they get to the laboratory that he was talking about. As Nick looks down he sees the doctor speeding up as he heads toward the fence. "Oh no you don't", Nick says as he smiles and heads down and fires a few pulses and takes out the gate.

"YEAH", Nick exclaims as he puts his hand into a fist and bends his elbow as he pulls it down.

Landing by the building Nick gets out and looks around. As the doctor stops the truck and gets out he asks, "What the hell were you doing? Playing with all the gadgets? I saw you firing those green energy pulses", Sam says as he smiles and starts laughing.

"I think those ones in the road were rather surprised... when I fired on them", Nick says as he laughs.

Coming over to them as they come out of the building, Jimmy and Bill ask, "What's so funny?"

"Hey... have you guys figured out how to fire the weapons on those things?" Nick asks as he points at one of the pods.

"I didn't know they had any", Jimmy replies.

"Well... he sure found them. Good thing too or we wouldn't be here right now", Sam says as they start walking to the building. Entering the front door of the building, they see all the lights on. They all follow the doctor down the hall as he turns left and then right as he takes them to the heart of the facility. As they enter the labs he looks around. Sam walks over to some of the equipment and starts checking it out. "Hey Jimmy. Come over here", Sam says.

Walking over to the doctor he asks, "Yeah. What is it?"

"Where is that stuff that sprayed on you on the craft? I need a sample", Sam says.

Pointing at it Sam takes a sample and puts it under a microscope. "Oh good lord", Sam exclaims as he looks at it.

"What", Nick, Bill, George and Jimmy say in unison.

"According to the microscope these cells are mutating every 10 seconds. No wonder our bullets don't have any effect on them. And if Freon can hurt them then we need to find something that is small enough to put aboard one of their ships and fly it into the big ship and blow it up", Sam says to them.

"And where are we going to find this Freon or whatever you call it?" Jimmy asks.

"I know where", Nick replies. "In Orlando! There is a place that stores jet fuel and liquid nitrogen for the shuttle. We can go their and see if we can modify something they may have on site", as he sounds excited.

"Sounds good to me", Jimmy says.

Just then a female comes from out of another room and heads toward them. "What the hell happened to her?" Nick says backing away.

"I don't know but I have a feeling it's from these things", Sam says as he tries to back away and bumps up against a table.

Looking around real quick Sam moves to the left and backs up behind the table. As she comes forward Sam flips the table up and over in front of her. She bends down and throws it out of her way, as if it were a rag doll. As she continues toward Sam, Nick grabs a floor lamp and hits her over the head with it. As it hits it squishes through her head and her brains come splattering out… all over. "YUCHHHHHHH", Nick exclaims as he goes over to a corner and bends over as he vomits.

"Oh man", Bill says as he walks over to a corner and starts puking himself.

"Gross", Lewis replies as he starts retching too.

"Haahahahaha", Sam and Jimmy laugh as they watch Nick, Ken and Bill throwing up.

"Oh, Nick… by the way. I need to tell you something about Amy", Lewis says.

"What?" Nick asks in a kind of demanding tone.

"Well… She kind of looked like this one did. She was walking down the road naked… and I thought I recognized her. I was going to stop and offer her a ride, but when I saw those things sticking out of her, I floored it. There was no way I was giving her a ride", Lewis says as he kicks at an imaginary stone.

"Oh no. This has got to be a nightmare. There is no way this can be real. Watch this. I will wake up and none of this will have ever happened", Nick says as his eyes start watering.

"Hey... I didn't mean for you to find out this way...... but I had to tell you", Lewis says as he goes over and pats him on the back.

"No. It's not your fault... I knew she was sick but not like this", Nick replies as he wipes his eyes and gets a rather strange look in his eyes. He says, "I WILL KILL ALL YOU BASTARDS FOR WHAT YOU HAVE DONE TO THE ONE I LOVE", as he shakes his hand at some imaginary creature that might be standing in front of him.

Just then they hear something coming down the hallway, and it doesn't sound good. It sounds like there are a hundred of them coming. "Quick... everyone. We need to find a way out. Bill. You and Lewis check out the south of the lab, while Jimmy and Sam can go check out the north and I will look down the hall and let you know when they are here. Now go. We don't have much time", Nick whispers as he goes to the door and looks down the hall.

Going over and looking in the south portion of the building Bill and Lewis find nothing. Jimmy and Sam go to the other side and they find nothing. Bill and Lewis move to the West Side as Jimmy and Sam check out the East Side. Just then they hear Nick as he says, "Here they come. Holy shit. There are at least two dozen of them coming. Someone… tell me you found a way out", he asks as he tries to block the door.

Just then Bill and Lewis find an old access door for the piping. Opening it up Bill and Lewis climb in and tell the others to hurry up. "Hey guys", Lewis says just before going in. "Over here", he motions.

Going over to the access door Sam and Nick get in. As the creatures come crashing through the door Nick says, "Jimmy. Come on. Let's go", as he starts climbing down the ladder.

"I'm coming", Jimmy says as he starts crawling in and one of those things grabs his arm and tries to pull him out. Shaking his arm he slips his arm out of the light jacket he is wearing and escapes, as they start tearing the wall out. Climbing down the ladder they finally get to the bottom, only to find their way blocked by a concrete wall. Looking around Nick looks for something to use as a pick. Seeing nothing he swears, "Damn them son of a bitches", as he slams his fists against the wall.

Starting to crumble away as he slams his fists into it, he says, "Hey guys… use your hands and feet and see if we can get through", as he beats on it.

Kicking it a few times Jimmy finally gets a small hole going and keeps kicking it. As the hole gets bigger Nick looks up and sees the creatures coming down the ladder. "Hurry up guys. They are coming", Nick says as he helps kick the wall.

As the hole gets big enough to crawl through, Bill and Lewis climb through. Sam and Jimmy go next, as Nick waits for his turn. As the creatures are halfway down Nick climbs through the hole and pauses as he looks back through the hole and watches one of the creatures come jumping down. Turning around he hauls ass after everyone else. Catching up he says, "Get the hell out of dodge man. They're coming", as he runs down the pipe.

As Nick nears the end of the sewer pipe, he looks out and sees the ocean. As he is about to run and jump he goes over to the edge and looks down. It is only a short hop down. Jumping down Nick looks around. Not seeing any of those things or their pods, he tells them to hurry it up. As soon as they are all on the ground Nick says, "We need to get some of their ships. We have to make it to Orlando and we need their ships to take them out".

"The only way we can get some of their ships... is if we take a few of them out and take their crafts", Lewis says as he kicks a small stone along the ground.

"Hey... wait a minute. We need to go back and get my truck. It has all the Freon in it. We could sure use them to help us out", Nick tells everyone as he looks around.

"You are a crazy cracker", Bill says as they both start laughing.

"I may be crazy but I get the job done and done well", Nick replies.

"Yeah I bet you do. You probably think you are bad, to, huh?" Bill asks.

"Of course I'm bad. Why... I'm so bad, I make the world... look good", Nick says as he laughs a little harder.

"Okay. Let's get going and see if we can get your truck back", Jimmy says as he starts out.

"Okay...... Everyone... Can I have your attention please...? We need to get going before those things get here", Nick says as he catches up with Jimmy.

"Hey... Jimmy. Is something wrong?" Nick asks as he scratches his ass.

"No", Jimmy says. "Why. Do I look like something's wrong?" he replies.

"Sort of. I just figured maybe you didn't like me or something. Or maybe I pissed you off and didn't know?" Nick says explaining why he asked to begin with.

"No. I just hate this whole thing. It stinks badly and it's getting worse all the time. Do we even have a chance of making it?" Jimmy asks hoping Nick had the answer.

"I know it stinks man. And I think we have a chance so long as we don't get caught. If we get caught... well then... I guess we will all die", Nick says as if stating facts.

Crossing the road they go into the woods and make their way through the trees as they look for any of those things. As Jimmy and Nick are talking and laughing, they stop and are quiet. They look ahead and see the labs they were just at. Looking around Nick doesn't see his truck, but he does see half a dozen of those pods. Just then 15 of the creatures come from around the building and get into their pods. As all the pods but 3 take-off, they wait for a little bit and see if any more of those things come out. Not seeing anything for 5 minutes Nick gets up and runs to the place where the gate used to be, and runs behind a building. Looking around the corner he sees his truck still there and all the Freon is still in it. Not seeing any of those things he decides to run over to his truck.

As he gets to the rear bumper two more creatures come from the building from a door in front of the truck. Ducking down Nick slides under the truck and waits for them to do... whatever they are doing. Seeing one of them go to a pod the other one comes over to the truck and starts it up. As the truck starts moving Nick grabs onto the rear bumper and kicking his legs up and next to the gas tank, he wedges himself to the bottom of the truck.

As the other guys see him climb on underneath they decide to go over and take one or two of the pods. As they get near Jimmy and Lewis run into one and take off. Sam and Bill get into the other one and take off right after Jimmy does. Flying low but far enough away they follow the truck to see where it's going. As the truck approaches a vacant lot it pulls in and stops. They see the creatures get out and go to the beach. Bringing the pod down to the ground Jimmy lands in a patch of woods. Bill lands his pod next to Jimmy's and they wait to see what happens next. As Jimmy and Bill both get out they creep over to the edge of the trees and look at the truck.

As they are looking they see Nick let his legs drop to the ground and he climbs out. Looking around he gets in and looks for the keys. "Damn", he says.

As they watch Lewis comes out and asks, "What's up guys?"

"Nick is trying to take the truck… I think", Jimmy says.

As Jimmy watches he sees Nick go to the left front wheel well. Pulling his hand out Lewis can make out Nick saying, "Damn". Going back to the cab Nick pops the hood. Going around to the front of the truck he looks inside and pulls something out. Just then two of the creatures come over the hill, toward the truck. Nick lowers the hood and shuts it as he runs around to the driver's side. Jumping in he opens the box and grabs the key inside. As it opens and he starts to get the key out, he looks inside it and sees there is no key here... Sorry Charlie... is what he thinks as he gets out of the truck. As he runs away they follow. Raising one of its arms it fires a green energy burst that just misses Nick.

# CHAPTER 11

As Nick runs away he sees a green energy pulse go by. As it goes by he kicks up his speed and literally hauls ass out of there. Running into the woods on the other side of the street, he runs right into Lewis and knocks him over. As he gets up and rubs his head and chin where he hit Lewis, he says "Let's go. I will take one and Jimmy you take the other. The button like thing on the right hand side of the green button… it's the fire button. The little knob thing on the left-hand side… that my friend is the tracking device. Push it to lock onto a target and then it tracks and fires. Now let's go", he says as he runs into the craft with Sam in it.

Lewis follows Nick and they take off. As they go up they see the creatures looking up at them as Nick starts firing the energy pulses. Hitting one the other goes a little quicker as he is trying to get to the truck. Jimmy comes up beside him and takes the other one out with a well-placed shot.

As Jimmy kills the other one, Nick lands next to his truck and gets out. Running to the truck Nick grabs two cans of Freon and takes them to the pod. As he keeps going back and forth, Lewis and Sam help out until all the canisters are aboard. Leaving his truck behind Nick, Lewis and Sam get back into the pod and take off.

As Nick flies it low to the ground he heads to Orlando where this place is. Jimmy follows Nick, as he seems to know where he is going. Just then, something happens and the pod Nick and Lewis are in starts spiraling downward. But it is going in slow motion almost. When it's 10 feet off the ground it smashes down and crashes. When their craft started spiraling down they all got into a safe position. When they hit it bounced them up and down. As they lie unconscious Jimmy brings his craft down and lands beside the crashed one. Getting out of his craft he goes over to the crashed one and tries to open the hatch. Looking and not finding any kind of release lever Jimmy sees four of the pods approaching. Trying to hide under the edge of the pod the crafts stop and start landing. "Oh shit", Jimmy says under his breath.

As the first one lands and two of those things get out, the door to the crashed one starts to open. "Yeah", Jimmy mutters to himself. Going in he sees Nick holding his head in his hands and Lewis lying unconscious. Grabbing a couple bottles of the Freon, Jimmy throws them out and onto the ground. As he goes out after the canisters he grabs one of the canisters and opens it up, as one of the creatures gets near him. Giving him a full face of Freon it stops dead in its tracks. As the others see their buddy stop they turn around and head back to their pods. Jumping out of the craft Sam and Bill each grab a tank and run over to the creature's pods. As they open them up they throw the open tanks of Freon into the pods. As the Freon fills the pods up with ice-cold air they come out and fall down. As they fall down Jimmy, Sam and Bill run over and freeze them. Not thinking right Jimmy runs over to the crashed craft. As he is about to go in Nick comes stumbling out. "Damn", he says as he appears in the hatch, "What the hell happened?" he asks as he gets out of the craft.

"Your pod started going out of control and you crashed. As I was trying to find out how to open the hatch, four of these pods came down and the creatures tried to attack us. We used your Freon to kill them, though. Are you feeling all right?" Jimmy asks.

"Yeah. I just bumped my head. It hurts like hell", Nick says as he winces in pain.

Going into the crashed craft Bill gets Lewis up and out of the pod. Taking him over by Nick they finally get their wits about them. "First off. Dr …Can you fly one of these?" Nick asks.

"I can try. I've watched you all long enough… to have a general idea", Sam replies.

"Okay. You and me… we'll go and take a test ride. Everyone else goes ahead and get in the other craft's and get going. Jimmy… you and Bill grab the Freon and put it in both your crafts. Now… let's get going", Nick says as he grabs Sam by the arm and they enter a craft.

Teaching Sam how to fly one he has the general idea of how to fly it. As they are landing everyone else is ready and waiting for them. After they land Nick gets out and goes over to the last one, just as 25 more of the pod like vehicles appear and start firing their green energy pulses. Jumping into his craft Nick takes off and engages the other pods and tries to draw their fire as he takes out two of them and starts flying across the sky. As 12 of the craft follow Nick, the others go after Jimmy, Lewis, Bill and Sam. Turning around Jimmy fires and takes out two of the craft. As Lewis turns around he starts firing on four of the ones tailing him. The green energy-pulses takes out one and the others fly by and bank as they head towards him. As they fly by Lewis rotates the craft and fires on them from behind and he takes out two more.

As Nick flies away he turns around and fires, as he takes out two more. They continue firing on him as he banks and turns as he tries to stay a moving target. As he starts getting too sure of himself, he slips up and he gets hit. As he is jarred from the hit he turns hard right and fires on the others. As he takes out four more he crashes in some trees. As the trees and water of the swamp cushion his fall, it is not as bad as the last one. Getting up, he staggers as his head clears, and then he jumps out of the craft and starts off, as fast as the knee-deep water will allow. Heading toward the trees not more than 50 feet away it seems like it takes forever to get their. Trying to dodge their energy pulses he finally gets to the woods. Stopping as he gets into them he catches his breath a little bit and starts running.

As he looks up he can see the crafts through little holes in the leaves. Running deeper into the trees he turns around as he hears a noise. As he turns back around he hits a low branch and it knocks him out cold. While Nick is laying their Jimmy, Sam, Lewis and Bill are having a tough time as well. As they take out half the ships Sam gets hit and goes down. Trying to avoid being pate he tries to bring the craft under some kind of control. Unable to bring it under control it crashes and explodes in a brilliant ball of flame.

Seeing the craft blow up Jimmy feels a sudden surge of adrenaline and starts taking the crafts out, until there are only two lefts and they run off in the direction of the big ship. As they regroup they land and discuss what they are going to do. "We will wait for ten minutes and then we go find him", Lewis says.

"I don't think that's a good idea", Jimmy replies.

"I don't care. If it wasn't for him… we would all be dead right now", Lewis says. "We can't just leave him out there", as he scratches his head.

"If we go and try to find him, we also run the risk of running into more of them. I say we head to Orlando and try to find this place he was going to", Jimmy says.

"Do whatever you want", Lewis replies getting irate. "I will go and find him by myself then. He's my best friend and I would never leave him out there… maybe all alone. If I know Nick and I do, he should have been back by now. So I'm going. Anyone going with me?" he asks.

"I will. I owe him a lot. He gave me job when no one else would. I would be dead if not for him", Bill says.

"Okay... I will go with you seeing as I don't know what I am doing or looking for. But we can only search for a short time then we have to go", Jimmy says as they get in their crafts and take off.

As they search for him they have no idea where he went. Looking down Lewis sees Nick's downed ship and heads for it. Landing near the craft Lewis gets out and looks inside. No one was around. Looking around he sees the trees only a short distance away. Closer than any other hiding places he thinks to himself. Pointing at the trees Jimmy and Bill fly over and try to look into the trees but they are too dense. Going to the edge of it Jimmy flies his craft under the trees so it won't be seen from above. Bill lands next to him and they get out. As they look around they can't see too far into the trees. Lewis walks to the trees and starts searching for Nick.

As Nick laid their unconscious a few people show up and take him to their hideout. "NICK", Lewis yells out into the woods.

As it starts getting dark Lewis and the rest agree to give up. Lewis said he knew where Nick was talking about. Flying to Orlando they run into minor disturbances. Once they get there, Lewis says, "These are the biggest tanks of liquid nitrogen that I know of. Now... we need to modify some cylinders and place them aboard the crafts".

They search around but to no avail. "Damn", Lewis says. "Wait a minute. Jimmy?" Lewis asks.

"Yeah", Jimmy replies.

"Have you had military training?" he asks.

"Yeah. Why?" Jimmy replies.

"Can you make some bombs if we can find the right stuff?" Lewis asks.

"Sure. Hey... wait a minute. I know where I can get all the stuff I need and can be back in twenty-five minutes", Jimmy suddenly exclaims.

"Bill you go with him. I will look around in this area for a store and see where I can pick up some headset radios, so we can keep in touch with each other. I'm tired of trying to figure out who's going where. See you when you get back", Lewis says as he heads for his craft.

"Okay. Be back in a bit", Jimmy says as he heads to his pod while Bill goes to his.

As they get into the different pods they take off and split up. Lewis goes over to the mall over by the trail. As he gets there he doesn't see any of the pod-like crafts around, so he figures it is safe to go in. Landing his pod outside, he gets out and walks into the mall. Trying to look around in the darkness, he tries to remember where the electronics places are. As he hunts and looks, he finds a toy store and finally finds a flashlight and batteries. Turning it on, he locates an electronics shop. As he looks for the better headsets, as he figures they will work better, he tries to carry them but finds out it is too much. Finding a small box, he loads it up with batteries and the headsets. Carrying them out to the craft, he gets in and closes the hatch. Just then the hatch opens back up and not waiting to find out who or what it was he takes off, as he hears a squeal come from below.

As the creature fires at Lewis he hits the ship, but does only minor damage as Lewis goes up and turns around and fires on the creature. As he fires he sees 4 more pod-like vehicles coming. Turning and taking off he heads in the opposite direction than what he really wanted to go. Leading them away Lewis finally loses them, when he goes into the cover of some trees. Watching as they pass overhead, Lewis waits a full five minutes and then takes off. This time he heads in the direction of the silo's that houses the liquid nitrogen.

Meanwhile as Lewis was having trouble of his own, Jimmy and Bill are having just as bad, if not a worse time. They got ambushed by 12 of the damned things. They were doing fine until they looked down and saw the pods waiting for them. Flying straight up Jimmy turns around and fires at them, before they get off the ground. Hitting three of them, he feels a little better. Diving low into the trees, Bill takes out two more. As Jimmy sees Bill going into the trees, he heads down into them as well. They probably can't navigate very well through trees.... Jimmy thinks.

Flying in and out of the trees Jimmy and Bill finally take out the last ship. As they continue on their journey they make it the rest of the way with no further interaction. As they land at the demolition place that Jimmy used to work at, they go inside and find everything he needs to make 8 bombs. As they are running out they are ambushed by a group of the creatures.

"SCREW YOU", Jimmy yells at the things, as he plugs a timer into a 12-ounce block of C-4 and tosses it at them, with only 4 seconds on the timer.

As it explodes it kills all the things that were coming for them. As they approach the pods they see one of the creatures coming out of it. Backing off they slowly back away and go to one of the other crafts. As Jimmy and Bill get into separate crafts, they take off. As Bill is flying away from the demolition place he hears a noise behind him and turns around. As he turns around he comes face to face with one of the creatures. Seeing the creature at such close range, Bill feints away and the craft starts spiraling down. As Jimmy looks out the window and sees Bill's craft spiraling down he knows something is up. It straightens out and then Jimmy thinks.... Maybe it was a glitch. He probably lost control for a second. Maybe he got his foot stuck... Trying to convince maybe himself more than anything else.

He sees the craft follow him to where they were supposed to be. As he flies he gets a bad feeling in his gut, but he ignores it. As they approach the nitrogen plant, they land and Jimmy gets out. As he waits for Bill, he starts getting nervous. Lewis approaches from out of the building and sees the creature, as it comes out and starts firing its energy bursts at Jimmy. Jimmy rolls to the side and rolls underneath a truck. Lewis sees all this and goes back into the building and gets a fire extinguisher. Taking it outside he sneaks around a tree and waits for the creature to come by. Peering around the tree he looks right into the creatures' twisted face. Pointing the nozzle at the creature he squeezes the handle, but it won't squeeze. The creature grabs him by the arm as Lewis takes the pin out and pushes the nozzle of the extinguisher in its face and squeezes like he never has before. As it sprays on the creature it lets Lewis go.

As it turns around Lewis squirts some in the other face. It writhes and squeals in pain and agony. Seeing what it does to them Jimmy runs inside and finds a fire extinguisher. Running back outside he sees that Lewis has the creature on the ground, covered in white foam. Jimmy runs over to the craft that Bill was in and sees if he is all right. As he enters the craft he sees Bill in the corner… unconscious. Going over to him he slaps his face and says, "Hey Bill. Wake up".

As he opens his eyes and shakes his head he says, "What the hell happened?"

"I guess you had a creature in your pod…… and he kind of took you out for awhile. You feel all right Bill?" Jimmy asks.

"Yeah. I'm fine", Bill replies as he rubs his temples.

"It didn't take me out" Bill fesses up. "He was in the pod, then I turned around and saw him in my face, I sort of feinted man. I'm not a hero. I didn't do anything… I choked… I guess I'm not good enough for you", Bill says as he looks down at the ground.

"Hey buddy. You did what your body wanted to do. It isn't your fault", Jimmy tells him as he pats him on the back". I have seen bigger men than you feint for things not as scary or horrible. Take it easy on yourself".

"Hey. Thanks Jimmy. I needed that", Bill replies, as he smiles.

# JANUARY 3, 2013
# CHAPTER 12

As Nick turned around at the noise, he hit a branch and got knocked out. As the noise moves closer it bends over and picks Nick up. Taking him to the hideout they lay him down on a bed and Brandy proceeds to try and revive him. As he starts to open his eyes and regain consciousness, he gets up on his hands and tries backing away. As his vision clears he sees they are humans... not those things...
Ahhhhhhh......... As he breathes a sigh of relief and lies back down.

"Hey dude", Robert says as he shakes him lightly.

"Stop it. Damn... let him rest a little bit before you go asking him questions", Brandy says as she scowls at him.

"Sorry", Robert replies as he starts backing away.

"W-What happened?" Nick asks as he starts coming around from Robert shaking him.

Robert goes over to Nick's side and says, "We saw you get shot down. You were in one of their crafts", Robert explains. "Then we saw you running through the woods and when Sonny here stepped on a branch… you looked around and hit your head as you ran into a low branch".

"Hey, I'm sorry dude", Sonny says as he looks down in shame.

"That's all right, Sonny", Nick replies as he tries to smile. "Where are we anyway?" he asks.

"We're in a warehouse where we can house the crafts we have taken into custody", Robert says as everyone but Nick starts laughing. "Sorry dude. Private joke", Robert apologizes.

"Hey, no problem. By the way, my name is Nick not dude man?" Nick says as he starts laughing at his own private joke. "Sorry man private inside joke", Nick replies as he bursts out, into another fit of laughter.

"Okay Nick. I am Robert and this is Brandy. She is the medic. And over there", as he points, "Is Johnny and Julio. And on my right, is Jessica. And you have already met Sonny", Robert says.

"Hi. Glad you guys were around", Nick says as he smiles at them.

"Hi Nick", they all say in unison.

"First things first", Robert says. "Do you have any idea as to how we can kill these things off?" Robert asks.

"Yeah. As a matter of fact me and my group…"

"Hey that was the other people we saw", Jessica blurts out as she interrupt's Nick.

"As I was saying...... I and my group were going to a plant in Orlando, as there is a liquid nitrogen storage facility there. Then we were going to"... As he explains the whole plan to the group.... "And then we were hoping if that worked out, you would be our back-up team. But... if we didn't find anyone else then we were going to do it and hope it works out right", Nick says as he scratches his head. "By the way. Is there anywhere I can clean up and maybe...... As he raises his eyebrow... Something to eat?" Nick asks.

"Yeah, sure", Robert says. "Johnny, take him to the shower we made up. And Jessica... Will you and Brandy please make something for lunch?" Robert asks as he smiles at Jessica.

Smiling back at him she looks at Brandy, who nods as she smiles and says, "Yeah, sure, Bob", she says as she starts laughing.

Johnny takes Nick to the shower and he washes himself as he gets the grime and dirt from the last day and a half off his body. Washing his body he thinks about Amy and starts crying, because there is nothing he can do to save her. He vows that if it comes down to it, he will do his best to make sure everyone else got away safely, before he does what he has to do. I have nothing left anyway. Why does this always happen to me? He asks himself. I try so hard to do the right thing and it always goes so bad for me. As he finishes he is over his crying jag. Drying off he puts his dirty clothes back on. As he walks out he says to Johnny, "A lot of good a shower does, when you have to put your nasty, dirty clothes back on", as he starts laughing at the humor of the situation.

"We have some clean clothes. You should have asked", Johnny replied as he starts laughing.

Laughing as they enter the main warehouse Robert asks, "What's so funny you two?"

"Oh, nothing", Nick says, "Private joke", as they burst out laughing again.

"Okay. It's almost dusk. We need to get some food loaded up. We have only four pods right now", Robert says. "Okay... Brandy... you and Jessica get the food. Johnny... you and Julio get the pods prepped for take off. Nick... you and Sonny are with me. Let's go", he says sternly as they begin moving. "We don't have much time".

"Robert.... What do you need me to do?" Nick asks.

"First, we need to get some Freon in case we can use it to get some more of their crafts. Then, when we come back, everything should be ready and we will go and see your friends", Robert explains. "Is that what you wanted to do?"

"Yeah sure. Is there an a/c shop around anywhere or do you know?" Nick asks.

"I'm not sure. I was going up to see my parents up north, when I checked into a motel and that was when shit started hitting the roof", Robert says.

No one else knows of anywhere so Nick says, "Well if we can't find one here we will have to find one en route to Orlando... Okay?" he asks.

"Yeah, I'm with you", Robert and Sonny say together.

"Okay. Let's go see what we can find. I figure an hour should be enough time", Nick says as he starts leading them down the road, in search of an a/c supply house or repair center.

As they look the others get the pods ready and loaded for the trip. They get about 2 miles down the road but they find nothing they can use. As they head back 3 pods shoot at them. Running into the woods, they scatter. Once they scatter they all look for anything to use for a weapon. As they run and look the pods land and the creatures come out and after them. Thinking for a minute Nick says to himself... I know what to do... And he smiles to himself inside. As he runs through the woods he goes around in a circle and gets behind the creatures. Then he starts running and gets into one of the pods and takes off. As he lifts off the creature starts shaking and splitting.

"Oh no you don't, you bastard", Nick mumbles to himself as he fires the weapons and takes it out, just as the split is complete. "YES", Nick yells to no one in particular.

Taking a chance Nick flies into the woods and sees one of the creatures, as it chases Sonny. Sonny is running and it is almost on him. Taking careful aim so as not to hit Sonny, Nick fires a round and gets the bastard. Landing so Sonny can get in, Nick takes off and they proceed to look for Robert. As they look it is almost dark out. Pointing ahead Sonny says, "There he is. Look. What the hell is it doing?" Sonny asks Nick.

"He is splitting into two creatures Sonny. Oh, I see. You haven't seen that yet?" Nick says as he starts laughing.

"No... I haven't. That's sick man", Sonny says as he starts making puking sounds.

"Hey, hey, none of that shit here", Nick says as he starts laughing again. Getting into range Nick fires the weapon again and takes the last one out, (after 7 shots of course).

Landing, Nick opens the hatch and Robert comes running up to the pod and gets in. "Well... we have three more pods if we can use them", Nick tells Robert.

"Hell yeah. That now gives us one each. Now to get back to the warehouse and show the others what we have acquired", Robert says as he smiles.

Getting them out of the woods Nick lands the craft and let's Sonny and Robert out, so they can take the other ones. As they get back to the warehouse, the others are all waiting for them. As soon as Robert gets out, Brandy comes up and says, "Where the hell have you guys been? We have been waiting for 2 hours. You were only supposed to be gone an hour?" as she looks him in the eyes and gives him a mean look.

Giving her an even meaner look he replies, "We got ambushed by a few of these things. We have the last pods we need to get our job done. So... no more bullshit and let's get the hell out of here".

"Okay, everyone lets go", Nick says as he gets back into a pod. Before closing the hatch he leans out and says, "Hey Robert?"

Robert looks out and sees Nick and gets out and says, "Yeah?"

"Follow me. If we don't find any place before hitting Kissimmee then we'll stop at my place, where I have about 90 cans of freon stockpiled from when I got a special deal on it", Nick says hoping Robert will agree.

"Okay", Robert replies as he gives Nick the thumbs up and gets into his pod and takes off.

Nick gives Robert a thumbs up and takes off at the same time that Robert does. Turning around Nick heads to Orlando. Not having any problems on the way they don't find anything and Nick takes them to his house. As he lands he notices the door to the garage open. Getting out of his pod, Nick walks over to the garage slowly to see if there are any of those things in here. Not seeing anything or anyone he motions for the others to go ahead and come on in. As they load all the cans into the pods, Robert carries the last two. As he closes the doors and locks it he feels a hand on his shoulder. "Yeah. What do you", he starts to ask when he turns around and sees Amy there, with things sticking out of her. Jumping back he tries to avoid her. Robert seeing what is happening comes over and is just about to hit her over the head with a can of Freon when Nick holds his hand up and says, "Wait a minute there Robert. This is my fiancé... or... whatever's left of her. Just all of you... leave... I am going to run to my pod and take off before she can get me", Nick says.

They all get into their pods and Nick leads her around in a circle and runs to his pod and gets in. Just as he takes off he sees her hands hanging on to the edge of the hatch. Once he gets about

15 feet off the ground, he starts going up and down letting her feet touch the ground. After doing this for a few minutes she finally lets go and he joins the others. Taking off Nick leads them to Orlando and the place he told them about. As they get there they circle and then proceed to land.

CHAPTER 13

**Aboard the big ship;**
Commander Knightwarp is pacing back and forth and in a very foul mood. Nothing is going like it was supposed to. Just then, Krulgerin walks in and bows before the commander. "My Commander, Knightwarp. I am sorry... but I have failed you. Do to me what you will", he begs slovenly.

"Get up Krulgerin. I need you for the time being. You are the only one that knows how to manipulate the doorway. Without you, we can't get back to the other planet and get our peoples out and over here. Now, get up and make sure those last humans are taken care of", Knightwarp demands.

"Yes, Commander Knightwarp. As you wish", Krulgerin says as he claps his hands and stomps his feet twice. Turning around, he leaves relieved he wasn't killed on the spot. As he turns

Knightwarp kicks him in the behind and says in a nasty, evil way, "I Want them gone........NOW".

As he walks down the corridor to his bunger, (private quarters), he is thinking to himself... So... I can do almost anything and he can't get rid of me because I am the key to the doorway... as he laughs to himself. He nods his head and Special Commander Jinforin appears around the corner and stops him. "So... what are you nodding and so happy about?" he asks.

"Oh, I was thinking how this is just great. We are winning the war with the humans. Now that all the females have mutated and taken out a lot of the males, we can take out the last few million males, who are trying to fight. HAHAHAHA", Krulgerin laughs.

"It is not going that well. We still have some... which are actually causing us some significant damage. If you can't take care of them, I will Krulgerin", Jinforin states.

"I will take care of them you smug son of a human", Krulgerin replies giving him an, I dare you look.

"How dare you call me that, you.... You human fleshbag. If you ever call me that again, I will kill you and the consequences can't be that bad", Jinforin states with an almost lethal stare.

"Smug son of a human", he breathes under his breath, as he turns and walks away from Jinforin.

Just then Jinforin turns to him and fires at his back and kills him instantly. Smiling to himself he walks to the command control and enters. "Well. I took care of Krulgerin for you, Commander Knightwarp", as he bows down.

"YOU WHAT", Knightwarp shouts at him. "You ignorant fool. He was the only one who knew how to open the gate. You will die for this mistake Jinforin", Commander Knightwarp says as he calls for 2 guards and tells them to take Jinforin away.

As he is being dragged away he is saying, "But my Commander. I did it for you. I thought that is what you wanted..." his voice cuts off, as the doors close.

Slamming his fists into a console, it catches fire for a few seconds and then goes out. "SON OF A HUMAN", he yells at no one. "I WILL KILL ALL YOU HUMANS IF IT IS THE LAST THING I DO", he continues to yell.

As Dinforst enters he is skeptical on whether he should stay or leave as he sees Commander Knightwarp slamming his fists on everything. "Ummmmm... Commander Knightwarp... I am reporting as you wanted", he says as he bows.

"What is it you want to tell me, Dinforst? That you know how to open the doorway?" Commander Knightwarp asks.

"Ummmmm... Well... Not... Only Krulgerin knows that. I only know what frequency it uses, but not for how long, or at what time precisely Commander", Dinforst says, as he lowers his head.

"Get up Dinforst. I need you to find out how to open the gates. As of now, you are the only one who has any idea as to how to open the doorway. Now go and report back when you have an answer for me. I don't want you to report until you find a way to open it. Now go and be gone, before

I turn around or you will be the next thing I hit", Knightwarp orders.

"Yes my Commander Knightwarp", Dinforst says as he claps his hands and stomps his feet twice.

As Dinforst is leaving, Stiderion enters and says, "My Commander Knightwarp. I am here to report as ordered", he says as he bows down.

"Get up Stiderion and give me your report", Knightwarp demands.

Standing up Stiderion starts his report and tells him things are not going as they had planned. "We are having trouble with some small groups of humans that are taking our forces out. We need some more reinforcements. They have taken out 1/3 of our forces and they keep getting our pods. If there is anything you can suggest… it would be most appreciated my Commander".

"You must group our forces and take them out a few at a time then. Krulgerin, the key to the doorway was killed and we have no way of opening it again unless Dinforst can come up with something. For now… regroup and make some plans so we can have the planet to ourselves again. Now go and don't fail me Stiderion. I will be keeping my eyes on you. Be off and DON'T report back until you have all the humans under control or annihilated", Knightwarp orders as Stiderion claps his hands and stomps twice.

As Stiderion leaves Knightwarp is still upset that everything was going so good until they started losing control and getting beat by humans. What a disgrace... Knightwarp thinks. I can't tell the High Lord Rothstrin that we are failing. He would laugh at me and have me put to death before my family in disgrace... As he hardens all his hands into fists. I vow to win this war, even if it means disgracing my family. I will kill them all... Knightwarp thinks.

## CHAPTER 14

As Jimmy, Lewis and Bill are looking up, they see 7 pods approach and circle. Thinking they are going to be ambushed, they scatter in all directions and wait to see. As the first pod lands, Nick gets out and says, "Where is everyone? Lewis... Jimmy... Bill... HELLO".

"I thought we were under attack again", Jimmy says as he comes out from hiding. "I thought you were a goner. Boy if you aren't a sight for sore eyes".

"So... are you Jimmy. I didn't know if you guys made it. Where is Sam?" Nick asks as he frowns.

"We lost him on the way here. We got ambushed......... and he got hit. His ship went down and exploded. Sorry to have to tell you that", Jimmy says as he walks over and pats him on the back.

"Well... I guess now we are going to do this for Amy, Sam and all the others we may have lost. We will kill them all and rid our planet of them.

Jimmy, Bill, Lewis, this is Robert, Jessica, Johnny, Julio and over there", as he points, "are Sonny with the hat and Brandy, the medic".

As they all shake hands and say hi to each other, they proceed to figure out how to make there plans work. Lewis says as he brings a box from his pod, "Hey guys. Check this out", as he brings the box over.

Handing out the headsets they check to see if they all work. "This is great. Who thought of this one?" Nick asks.

"I did", Lewis says as he smiles.

"Jimmy. You and George go and fly around a little bit and see how far they work away from each other. I will keep mine on and see when you get out of range", Nick says as he puts his headset on and checks it. Satisfied he starts asking questions and seeing if anyone can come up with some sort of an answer.

Giving them enough time to think of something he finally says, "Okay. Here's the plan", as he tells it to them all. As they all agree to what they are going to do, almost everyone gets into a pod and takes off. "Jimmy. You there?" Nick asks into the headset.

"This is Jimmy, go ahead Nick".

"How far away are you Jimmy? Did you hear the plan also?" Nick asks.

"Yeah Nick. We are about 2 miles away now. I am going to take Lewis and go find my special items. I will keep in touch and if you can't get me, then I am probably"... Jimmy goes out of range.

"Damn. Well... at least we know we only have 2 miles of communication to use. Anyway let's get busy guys and then we will do our damage", Nick says as he starts toward a building.

12 hours later everyone except Jimmy and Lewis make it back. "Okay... I see everyone was successful on his or her expedition. Good. We will need all the stuff you guys have. Has anyone heard from Jimmy and Lewis lately?" he asks.

As everyone shakes his or her heads no, he says, "Okay. Let's get busy and prepare for war people. Hop to it. You all know what needs to be done" Nick says as he walks over to one of the storage tanks and looks up at it and smiles. YES... He thinks to himself. We will succeed. I can feel it. As he goes to the ladder going up the side of it, he can hear a slow hissing sound coming from up the tank. Hmmm.... He thinks. Starting to climb up the hissing gets louder. Shaking his head he finally gets to what is making the noise. It is a pressure relief valve. Whew.... He thinks as he gets on the platform and waits for Robert to get up there with the hoses.

As Robert comes over he climbs up the ladder with about 100 feet of hose. Climbing the ladder he stops about halfway up and lets half of it fall to the ground. Catching his breath, he climbs up until he gets to the top. As Nick helps him up he rests for a minute and says, "That is one hell of a climb with all that hose to carry up. Next time, you get the honors", Robert says as he smiles.

"Okay. I don't give up so easy though", Nick replies sarcastically, as he starts laughing.

"Yeah. You go to hell too", Robert says as he starts laughing as well.

Finding the fitting he is looking for Nick yells down, "HEY... JOHNNY".

"YEAH", Johnny yells back.

"HOOK UP THE GAUGES TO THE HOSE", Nick replies.

"OKAY", Johnny says as he hooks up the gauges.

Nick hooks up the hose to a screw on fitting. As he screws it on a little bit escapes until the seal works. Taking a pair of pliers to the hose Nick tightens the hose end down, as tight as he can. "Okay. Let's go", Nick says.

Robert gets up and climbs down the ladder as Nick comes down right after. As they get to the ground, Jimmy and Lewis fly in and land. After landing Jimmy comes running out of his pod and runs over to Nick. "Guess what I found?" he asks Nick.

"You found a beautiful babe with big tits?" Nick replies jokingly as he starts to smile.

"No. Look", as he shows them what he got.

"WOW. That is exactly what we need to do some damage", Nick replies with a look of excitement on his face.

"Okay. Let's get the pods modified and see if we can check them out before going", Nick says as they all get busy and modify the pods and finish hooking up the hoses. Checking to make sure they all have gauges, he starts hooking the nose sprayers on. "Robert", Nick says.

"Yeah", Robert replies, as he sticks his head out of a pod.

"Are you any good at welding?" Nick asks.

"Yeah. I did my fair share of it. Need some help?" Robert asks.

"Yeah. I can rig up the nose sprayer but I need someone to weld them on as I set them up", Nick says.

"Okay. Coming", Robert says as he finishes what he was doing and then helps Nick.

As they continue finishing with the nose sprayers, they start attaching hoses to them and then torching holes in the hatchway area for the hoses to go through. As they get all the pods ready for the big one, Brandy and Jessica come back with a load of food for every pod. As they load the food into the pods Nick goes over and hooks up the first pod. Filling it to 350 psi, he asks Jimmy to go in the pod and check the lever to make sure it works. As Jimmy pulls the lever, liquid nitrogen starts spewing out in vaporous form. "Excellent", Nick and Jimmy say together as Jimmy comes out of the pod.

As they charge and check each one, they get them all in working order. That is when Nick wants to go back and recharge all the pods to 450 psi. Jimmy looks at him and raises his eyebrows, as he asks, "Is that safe?"

"Does it matter? I mean is what we are going to be doing safe? I don't think so", Nick replies smug as hell.

"You got me. Okay… let's go ahead and do it", Jimmy replies as they proceed to each and every pod.

As they get finished Nick looks at his watch and sees it is 5:30 a.m. "All right everyone. We need to hide our pods and tonight is when we go through with our plan. Okay", Nick asks.

"Okay", they all agree in unison.

As they each get into the pods, 5 other pods come down and land. Talking on his headset Nick says, "Okay everyone. This is it. Let's all go up and take'm out".

"Roger that Nick", Robert replies.

"Let's go", Nick says as he takes off and aims his pod down and starts firing as those creatures started coming out. As the nitrogen plant becomes a battlefield the creatures never had a chance. As they get done having fun and taking some more out, they go to a forest and take their pods into the trees. Taking turns standing watch they get rested up for their big day or rather night.

JANUARY 4, 2013
CHAPTER 15


As Stiderion tries to get the forces under control, he finds that none of his brethren are even paying attention. Most of them are in a fight for their existence. Looking down from his pod Stiderion can't believe what is happening. They are getting over run by the humans. Ordering all the forces by telepathy to congregate at these coordinates, Stiderion watches and waits. As a minimum of forces appear, Stiderion demands that they all go out and bring all the forces together, at these coordinates in 12 hours, or they will be left behind. As the small group goes out they tell all the forces the orders they received. Flying around the world Stiderion is most displeased with the progress.

As Stiderion looks at what forces are left he notices some of their own ships are being used against them. He decides on an option that shouldn't have come up. Once they gather he will tell them his entire plan. As he continues his flight he wonders what would happen if they lost. Shaking his head he flies to the coordinates. Landing he gets out and waits. Over the next 10 hours pods arrive and congregate. As the 12 hours is up Stiderion sees they have well over 3 million forces left. As two guards get his platform, he thinks for a minute. As they bring his platform over he steps aboard it. Flying around Stiderion starts his speech:

As you all know, we are losing this battle. We need order. You are going about this in the wrong way. First... I want you to separate every time you find another pod, I know this is not our way... but we have to go to extreme measures. Once we have doubled our forces, we can then concentrate on the humans. We need to get all our pods back. The humans are using them against us. Second... I want groups to go in force and annihilate every human you find. Third... If you fail... you will pay the price. We have to win. If we do not win we will become extinct. We can't allow that to happen. If you want to live then let's get out there and take out the humans as we are supposed to already have done. Now go and don't fail Commander Knightwarp... or your planet...... or your family will be disgraced from the junction. Go and be victorious, "he demands as he flies back to his pod.

Once the platform is loaded up Stiderion takes off and watches to see what is going to happen. I will not take defeat... he thinks as he slams his fists into the console. Watching, he sees that the forces are starting to organize and begin the annihilation. Shaking his head he watches as his forces start doubling themselves. Yes... He thinks to himself... We will win now so long as they continue with my orders. Liking what he sees he decides to go report back to Commander Knightwarp. Flying to the Bermuda Triangle he approaches the big ship and enters. As he lands his pod in the place reserved for him, he gets out and strides to command control. As he enters he sees Commander Knightwarp pacing the floor, talking to himself.

"My Commander Knightwarp. I bring you my report", Stiderion says as he bows at Knightwarp's feet.

"Stand Stiderion", Knightwarp says.

As Stiderion stands he says, "Commander... I have ordered the forces to annihilate the humans. They are looking to be successful. I have watched over them and I can say we will have total annihilation by tomorrow at this time".

"Very good Stiderion. If you keep this up you will be honored and revered when we finally take our planet back. You are proving to be a valuable asset to this annihilation. Now go... and make sure everything goes as planned. I will not tolerate failure and neither will the junction", Knightwarp says.

"Yes my Commander Knightwarp", Stiderion replies as he claps his hands and stomps his feet twice. Leaving he walks down the hallway and hears Jinforin yelling out, "I did it for you Commander. I only did what you really wanted. Please... don't disgrace my family. I can take the humans out for you. I can", as he bangs on the hatch door.

Smiling, (if you call what they do smiling), Stiderion continues down the walkway. Going to his bunger he enters and lies down exhausted from all the extra time he has been putting in. As he lies down, Kinglosin enters and asks, "Stiderion... If you give me the chance I will prove to you how good I am at leadership", he says in a begging sort of way.

"Very well Kinglosin. I want total annihilation in 6 hours. If you can do this, you will be well rewarded. Now go and check back with me when you have taken control of our planet", Stiderion says as he waves him away.

"I will not let you down Stiderion", Kinglosin says as he claps his hands and stomps his feet twice. Leaving he goes out and proceeds to carry out Stiderion's orders.

## CHAPTER 16

As Nick watches guard while everyone else is sleeping and getting rested up for tonight, he notices a swarm of pods heading in an easterly direction. I wonder where the hell they are going... he thinks. Looking at his watch he sees it is 5:00 p.m. Just a little while longer, in a couple of hours we are going to see if this plan works. I hope it does. If it doesn't, then may god have others out there that can! He thinks. As 6:30 rolls around Nick starts getting everyone up and ready. "Come on... Let's go... We need to eat and check our equipment and make sure everything is still working properly", Nick says as people start to get moving.

Once everyone has gotten up and they are awake, Nick takes Robert and Jimmy to the side. "We have got to make this work. If anything fails and someone has to stay behind, then it will be me. You guys make sure everyone else gets out alive, so we can be sure we have succeeded. Is this agreed?" Nick asks.

"Wait. Why does it have to be you? You are the best suited for leading these people... if we fail", Robert says.

"Yeah. Why not me or Robert?" Jimmy asks.

"Because. My whole reason for living... is now one of them. I can't go on without Amy and I won't, if it comes down to it. Now I don't want to hear no more. I want you guys to agree to my plan and make sure we succeed. Okay?" Nick asks them as he looks at each of them.

"Agreed", they say in unison but with sad looks on their faces.

As the others get dinner ready they go and start checking the sprayers and supplies. Checking to be sure that all the tanks are sufficiently full, Nick then checks the entire strap on tanks. Satisfied with their output he goes over and is just about to grab something to eat, when Brandy smacks his hand and says, "Not yet Mr."

"Okay, okay", Nick says as he rubs his hand where she hit him.

"Okay... everyone. This may be the last big meal we have so let's get together and have a prayer", Brandy says.

Once everyone gathers around Robert says, "Dear Heavenly Father... we thank you for all the time you have given us in life. We are grateful for all the new friends we have found... though it may be in stressful times. We thank you for giving us a chance to fight for our right to live and for a possible peace on our planet. As we pray to you this evening... we ask that you watch over all of us and the others that may still be alive out there. Bless each and every one of us as we try to take our planet back from whatever creatures that are trying to take it from us. Let us win this battle... for our rights as humans. May our plan succeed so we don't have to live in fear anymore... We beg you to please... let us be victorious in this battle that we will be going into this day. With all your greatness and Holiness, we bless you Father... Amen", he says as he finishes his blessing.

"Amen", everyone says as Robert says it.

Eating until they get full on food, they all relax for a short time because they know that they are going into a possible, one-way battle. They don't want to go into battle and get tired. As they get done Nick says, "Okay... We are going to bring our plan to life. We need everyone to do his or her part. As we get close to the objective, we will radio back at regular intervals so as to keep each other up to date on our progress. Now... does everyone know what they are doing?" he asks.

"Yes", he hears from all.

"Okay... let's get out there and kick some creature ass", Nick says as he goes to his pod and gets in.

As everyone gets into their pods Nick is already up in the air and going out to the open sky. As he gets there he sees thousands of the pods soaring overhead. "Everyone. We have a swarm of pods above us. I think this is going to be a part of the war we didn't think about. Let's attack", Nick says into his headset.

The instant they swarm out of the trees they are under attack. Attacking back, Brandy comes about and takes out two of the pods. Turning back around her pod is on a crash course for a tree. Trying to steer out of the way, she can't avoid it. Her pod crashes and burst into flames. "Come on people. Let's get to it. We can't afford to lose anyone else", Nick says as he takes out five more pods. Turning around he sees a group of tree's coming up and heads for them hoping the other pods will follow. As he goes into the trees, the other pods follow him but are not very good at flying in a forest, 6 of the 8 that went in, crash and burn. Nick comes out the other side and turns around. As they come out Nick fires on them and takes them out. "Yahooooooo", Nick yells into the headset.

"Hey… that's no fair", Robert says. "You can't take credit for the tree crashes", he says as he takes out another ship.

"What. I led them into the woods. They are creditable to my account", Nick replies back as he starts laughing.

"Okay. I suppose this time but that's it. No more", Robert replies as he starts laughing to.

Finally as they take out the last two they come together and land in another thicket of trees. As Nick gets out of his pod he says, "All right. Them-1. Us-28. I guess that's good enough for now. But we have to stick together and finish this mission out to the end. We can't lose any more of our people. Now… let's bow our heads and pray that Brandy is going to a better place than this", Nick says as he taps Robert on the shoulder and nods his head.

Robert knowing Brandy better than the others leads the prayer; Dear Heavenly Father, take care of Brandy and keep her safe. May we finish this task at hand... so you will see how much we want to survive. Bless our whole group as we continue on, in this battle. Amen", Robert says as he looks up.

"Amen", everyone else says in unison.

"Okay everyone. You all know what to do. Each group should keep in communication range. If we get lucky, then we will be hearing from each other. Now good luck and make it back safely", Nick says to all.

"Yeah. I will be back. Don't worry about that", Julio says.

"I will be back just so I can bug you a little more", Lewis says as he starts laughing.

"We will all make it back. Good luck to everyone. Let's do this right the first time, because there won't be a second chance. Now... let's go and kick some creature ass", Robert says as he goes to his pod.

Everyone wishes everyone else a safe journey and good luck as they go to their pods and get in. As Nick gets into his, he checks the radios, "Nick to all. Everyone read me okay?"

"Robert here. I read you loud and clear".

"Lewis here good buddy. See you at lunchtime", he says as he laughs.

"Johnny here. Good luck", he says as he runs a last minute check on his equipment.

"Bill here. Everything's fine".

"Sonny here, dude", as he laughs, "loud and clear".

"Jessica reporting in. I've got excellent reception. See you on the flip side guys", as she takes to the skies.

"Julio here. Take your time and let's kick ass", he says as he takes off.

"Jimmy here friend. You are coming in just fine. Have a good flight and thanks for flying killer express", he says as he starts laughing.

"Okay… let's go and do our duty for our planet", Nick says as he takes off and flies to the east.

Once they get over the ocean the crafts handle a little different. Must be the current on the surface of the water.... Nick thinks. As they approach the Bermuda Triangle they all see a bright green glow, coming from something yet it looks like it is holding something up in the air. Must be the ship the doc was talking about. I just never imagined it would be soooo, big... Nick thinks. "Well there she is guys. Our destination is straight ahead. This will probably be the last radio contact we have… until the job is finished. Good luck groups and let's party", Nick says as he flies to the West Side of it as Robert follows him.

Lewis and Jimmy head to the East Side as Lewis says, "Good luck buddy. See you around".

Jessica and Julio veer over the top of it and come in from around back.

Johnny, Bill and Sonny head for the front center, figuring they could do better from there, unless they see a better place to land.

"Good luck all and happy hunting", Jessica says as she loses contact after reaching the crest of the big ship.

"Good luck bossman. Enjoy your time here", Bill says and starts laughing as he goes out of range.


As Nick and Robert close in on the ship they lose all communications with the other groups. Intent on their goal they fly into the ship and look for a dock. As they fly around inside, he notices there aren't any pods around. That's strange… he thinks. "Nick to Robert, you copy, over".

"I copy you Nick. Go ahead, over", Robert replies.

"I see where we're headed. It doesn't look too friendly either. Are you ready to have some fun, over", Nick says as he heads toward the west dock.

"Roger that Nick. See you when we land", Robert replies, as they fly into the dock and see about 50 of the creatures standing around.

As they enter the creatures look at their pods, as if they weren't supposed to be there. As they pull weapons from their sides they start firing. "Let's take'm out Robert. Ready ... Set... Fire", Nick says as they pull their levers and coat the dock with nitrogen.

As it hits the creatures they start freezing instantly. Rotating his pod Nick makes sure there are no more left here. Satisfied he lands his pod. As he gets ready to get out he puts on his twin cylinder pack and opens the valve wide open and ready for combat. As Nick gets out of his pod,

Robert lands and gets out of his too with his pack on. Giving Robert the thumbs up Nick goes to the door and notices it takes some kind of special rod to open it. "Robert. We need some kind of rod or key to open this door", Nick says.

"I'll look over there and you search here", Robert replies.

As they search they finally find something that Nick says may work. Putting the rod into the hole, the door opens. As the door opens 15 creatures start coming in, firing their weapons. As Nick sees the creatures coming in, he ducks down and rolls to the side as he lets them have a blast of instant freeze. As they slow down and freeze some of them drop their weapons. After the last one is froze Nick reaches down and picks up a weapon. Motioning for Robert to come on, Robert picks up a weapon too as they start a relay procedure as they go down the hall.

As Jessica and Julio fly over the top of the ship, they discover hundreds of pods waiting in ambush. Waiting for them to go into the dock. Turning her pod around as quick as she can Julio follows her and asks, "What are you doing? I thought we were going to come in the back door?"

"We were… until I saw hundreds of their pods on the other side… waiting in ambush. So… let's take them by surprise. You go to the right and I will go to the left, and we will catch them in crossfire, over", Jessica says.

"I will be waiting for you in the middle, so don't be late", Julio replies with a sarcastic tone to his voice.

"Okay. I will meet you in the middle after we take out the ambush party, Lets rock and roll Julio", Jessica says.

"You got it Jesse", Julio replies as he starts heading to the right and heads around the big ship.

As Julio goes to the right he sees the ships and stays out of sight as he gets to where, when he starts firing he will catch the most of them. Waiting for Jessica to get into position, he radio's her, "Jessica. I am ready and waiting for your go".

"If you are ready so am I. Let's do it Julio", Jessica says as they both head in with energy pulses blazing away. As they take out 3, then 4, then 5, Jessica takes a hit and her pod starts diving crazily.

Thinking this is another human trick thirty of the creatures follow her and shoot as they pursue her. Gaining control of her pod, she turns around and fires off 8 quick bursts and makes contact with 4 of the other pods. As her pod gets shakier by the minute she says, "Julio. I have been hit and am going in to a docking bay. Do what you can and I will start the assault on the big ship. Over", Jessica says as she heads for a nearby dock.

"I will be right behind you. I have taken out 23 of the bastards so far", Julio says as he dives and turns around and fires a shot in all directions now that he knows Jessica is gone. As his pod gets swarmed and he gets caught in the middle he tries to contact Jessica, "Jesse. I am in a no-win position. I am going to blow my pod up and take as many as I can. Tell everyone I said good luck and if you ever meet my family, tell them that I did the right thing for a change. Good-bye Jesse... it has been fun knowing you", Julio says as he goes back and sets his timers for 10 seconds. As he avoids the pods he pulls the lever and turns around crazily as he sprays everything that gets in front of him.

As Julio sprays them he notices the pods are trying to get him in the center of all of them. Deciding to make them think they succeeded he looks at the timer and watches as the timer fades down. 3... 2... 1... As Julio's pod explodes in a fierce fireball, it is like letting an atomic bomb loose without the radiation though. It makes a fiery ripple that destroys everything in its path. As the pods start exploding one by one, there are only 15 that make it. As Jessica hears Julio's last words she tried to contact him, but he must have taken his headset off. "DAMN", she yells as she realizes this battle is far from over. With renewed vengeance she lands and sprays the nitrogen vigorously as she enters the dock. Landing she puts on her twin cylinders and gets ready to go out.

As Lewis and Jimmy are flying around the East Side, they find their dock with no problem or any conflict. As they land they look around and see no one around. Getting out with his gear on Lewis walks out and looks around. Motioning for Jimmy to come out he exits his pod with his tanks on as well. Going to the door they find it locked and they can't figure out how to open it. "I got it", Jimmy says as he runs to his pod. Just before getting in he tells Lewis to step out of the way. "I am going to shoot it open. Just be ready for any of those creatures that may come out", Jimmy says as he lifts the pod 3 feet off the ground and aims at the door. Firing the energy pulse it blows the door outward and kills 5 creatures, which were waiting on the other side.

"I guess they weren't expecting that... huh... Jimmy?" Lewis says as he starts to laugh.

"No. I think they thought we would give up, and then they could ambush us", Jimmy says as he lands the pod.

Getting out, Lewis is already in the hallway and looking down it. As Jimmy joins him in the hallway, they proceed down the corridor and keep an alert eye out for creatures. As they are walking down the corridor they come to a 3-way junction. "Okay. I will go this way", Lewis says as he points down a corridor and says, "and you take that one and when we get out of range of each other we will report back. If I get into trouble I will head back if I can. If I can't, I will run like hell until I can get back to you. Take it easy and have fun", Lewis says as he walks down the corridor, with his nozzle ready to go.

"Okay. Let's meet back here in 5 hours... if nothing else. Then we will go down this last corridor... together. Have fun and let's party", Jimmy says as he walks down one of the other corridors.

While Lewis walks down the corridor he gets the creepy feeling that he is being followed. Turning around he sees a creature coming at him from a secret door. Turning his nozzle toward the creature he is too slow and the creature knocks him down. Grabbing the nozzle again, Lewis aims up and let's the nitrogen fly as it freezes the creature instantly, just as he was about to smash his head in with a pipe. "Whew", Lewis says as he wipes his forehead. "I just had my first encounter Jimmy. Watch out for secret doors. He tried to ambush me. Didn't work though… Hahahaha", Lewis says as he laughs.

"Hey… thanks for the warning buddy. Keep in touch dude", Jimmy says.

"Yeah. I will. Have fun and don't get lost", Lewis replies.

As Jimmy goes down his corridor he sees it branch off into 3 more sections. Sticking to the left one he continues down the corridor. As he peers around a corner he comes face to face with one of those creatures. Raising his nozzle, he sprays the creature in the face. As the creature is about to squeal, his face is frozen in a macabre way. As he looks at it Jimmy starts laughing as the funniness hits him. Searching the creature he finds a weapon and some rods. Pocketing the rods he puts his nozzle behind him and totes the weapon in his hands.

"Lewis… you there?" Jimmy asks.

"I'm right here buddy. Where are you at?" Lewis asks.

"I have taken two left turns and run into a few of the creatures. I am heading back in 25 minutes, over", Jimmy says.

"I will be waiting for you. I kind of came up on a dead end. I am heading back now, over", Lewis replies.

When Johnny, Bill and Sonny headed to the north side of the ship, they were up to their necks in creatures. As soon as they got to the interior of the craft, about 35 pods came out of secret doors. As they fought trying to stay alive, they ended up taking out the dock in the center of the ship. As it explodes in brilliant flames Johnny gets a little too close as his craft is shaken like a rag doll. As his craft is spinning crazily out of control, Johnny grabs the C-4 and timer and opens the hatch as he says into his headset, "If anyone is near me, get your ass over here now… cause I am going to jump".

Bill being the closest goes over and under Johnny's pod. Just as he gets underneath his pod Johnny jumps and lands on the front of Bill's pod. As Johnny jumped, the damaged pod hit the core pylon and bounced off, as it came right by Bill's pod and just missed taking Johnny off the pod. As Johnny turned to look he saw the nose of his pod come to within a foot of knocking him off. As Johnny watches the pod careen out of control, bouncing off things as it goes down, it explodes with a tremendous blast and takes out part of the core pylon. As Bill was trying to avoid all obstacles he continued firing his energy pulses. As the explosion went off Bill's pod was buffeted around slightly, as the warm rush of hot air blew upward. When the explosion occurred, 8 of the enemy pods were taken out.

Flying low but high enough to hit them, Sonny comes up from underneath a troop and takes them out as he goes through the explosion of one and his craft hits a piece of debris from it and starts spinning down out of control. Grabbing his C-4 with the timer already in it he sets the timer for 20 minutes, (he was trying for seconds), when his craft crashes into the lower deck and explodes in a huge fireball as it takes out part of the ship.

Shaking the others off his tail Bill lands in a dock on the north side, as Johnny jumps down and gets behind the pod. The creatures on the dock open fire on them. Johnny runs behind a pile of can type things and hides as he says, "Okay Bill. Let'em have the nitro. Now".

"You got it Johnny", Bill says as he lets the creatures have a blast of ice cold nitrogen vapors.

As they started freezing Johnny started getting cold and says, "B-B-Bill.... Y-y-you... N-n-need... To-o-o.... Get ov-ov-over here… N-n-now".

"I'm their buddy. Hold on for a sec", Bill says as he lands near where Johnny is. "Sonny… you there?" Bill asks. Not getting a reply he asks again, "Sonny… you there?" "Damn", Bill says as he lands.

Landing and jumping out Bill helps Johnny onto the side of the pod. As Johnny warms up he says, "I hope the rest of the guys are doing better than us".

"Oh I'm sure they are. I can't get a hold of Sonny. I think we lost him too", Bill says as he gears up for combat.

Getting off the craft they head for the door that used to be there. Looking around the corner Bill starts down the hall. While Johnny follows Bill he stoops down and picks up one of the creature's weapons. Looking at it he points it in what seems the right way. Heading down the corridor they come to a split, but decide to stay together. "Two people are better than one", Bill says as they continue making their way to the core of the ship.

# CHAPTER 17

Landing in the big ship Kinglosin goes to Stiderion's bunger and sees if he is there. Not finding him there he heads to command control. As he gets to the command control, Commander Knightwarp is in a most foul mood. Entering Kinglosin says, "My Commander Knightwarp... I have come for my report", he says.

"I don't want your report right now. We have a bigger problem at hand. We have intruders aboard and they are taking out our forces...... much too fast. Now go and find them and annihilate them all. I will not tolerate failure Kinglosin. Now go and don't come back 'til you've annihilated all intruders", Knightwarp says as he paces back and forth. "Lock all doors and seal all docks", he says as he continues pacing. "You are still here?" Knightwarp states as he sees Kinglosin still bowed down.

"Sorry my commander", Kinglosin replies as he gets up and leaves, not bothering with the traditional salutation.

Walking down the corridor Kinglosin can hear Jinforin yelling out crazy thing's from his cell. Not bothering with him, he continues down the corridor when he runs into Stiderion. "Stiderion… we have intruders aboard. The Commander wants us to shut all docks and seal all interior doors", Kinglosin says.

"I will notify all our forces in the western section and you go to the eastern section and spread word as you go, as will I", Stiderion orders as he starts toward the western section.

Kinglosin heads to the eastern section and runs into Jimmy, who fires before he has a chance to do anything. "YES", Jimmy says as he tells Lewis that he just took out another creature.

"That's another one for our side", Lewis says as he asks, "Do you need me there? If not, I am going to head your way and take a different corridor. One that we have not explored yet".

"Okay. Just let me know what corridor you go down so I can join you later", Jimmy replies.

"Okay. See you in a bit", Lewis says as he goes the way Jimmy went.

As Stiderion heads to the west he tells everyone he sees that all doors should be locked, and all docks sealed. As he comes to the block central he opens the hyperdoors and enters the hyper-terminal. Going down to the docking section Stiderion goes to each dock, and tells them to lock down as there are intruder's aboard. As he comes to some of them he notices that they have pods in them, and there are some of his species dead. Hitting the wall as he walks out of the first one he encountered he does the same thing at each one he finds.

Heading to the engine deck Stiderion runs into Dinforst. "Dinforst we have intruders aboard. We need to lock all docks and seal all doors until they are caught".

"Okay. I am going to the labs to see if we can open the doorway again. I think I found out how to open the doorway whenever we want to. I will tell everyone I see", Dinforst replies as he continues down the hall toward the labs.

Stiderion continues his trip through the ship, telling everyone and locking doors as he goes through them. Once he gets to the engine room he tells everyone to be prepared for intruders. Get your weapons… and don't let anyone near the cores. Leaving he goes back to the upper levels and goes to his bunger. Once inside he gets out the special weapon he had made just for this occasion. Loading the snerls into it he pushes a button and arms it. Now that he is ready for battle, he goes back out into the corridor and starts down it as he heads in the opposite direction as he came from.

## CHAPTER 18

As they went down the corridor they came to a split but decide to stay together, as they really can't afford to get separated. Not when two people can help each other out in the long run. Taking the right-hand corridor, they head down it. Hearing something up ahead, they flatten themselves against the wall and try to blend in. Further down the corridor, as a door opens, a troop of 12 creatures comes out and heads down the corridor, toward Nick and Robert. "Whenever you are ready, we will take them out", Nick says in as low a voice as possible, so Robert can still hear him over the headset.

"I'm ready. Let's go.1... 2... 3... NOW", Robert says as they both step out and start firing at the creatures.

As the creatures start falling one by one, they take out the whole troop. Not seeing anymore they head down the corridor and proceed with caution. As Nick looks to the front for a few seconds, a green energy pulse hits him from behind. Falling down, Robert sees him and comes over, "What happened?" Robert asks.

"I got hit from behind. Go on. I will take care of your back", Nick says as he pulls out the C-4 and timer and gets ready to use it.

"I am not going to leave you here to die. I am going to make sure you live, to make it out. You have been the best leader any of these guys could ever have", Robert says.

"Don't worry about me. Remember the objective. Finish what we started. I can take care of the creature's back here. Now go", Nick says as he fires a couple of quick bursts down the corridor.

"I will be back for you... When I find what we are looking for, I will be back to get you. If you are still here, I will get you out, don't worry", Robert says as he starts to leave.

"I will be waiting if I can", Nick replies as he smiles.

Robert continues down the corridor as Nick lies on the floor. Waiting for the creature that hit him, Nick decides to play dead. As 3 creatures come down the hall after Robert, Nick waits 'til they are past him and opens fire on them, taking them all out. "I gott'em for you buddy", Nick says as he gets up and heads the way Robert went. "Where are you at Robert?" Nick asks.

I went to the left at the next intersection. I will wait for you", Robert says as he finds a place to hide.

"I'm on my way. Be there in a sec", Nick says as he heads to the left at the next intersection. As he walks down the corridor, Robert grabs him as he walks by. Feeling something grab him, Nick turns quickly and gets ready to fire a round off, until he sees its Robert, "Don't do that. I almost fried you", Nick says as he lowers his weapon.

"Sorry. I forgot where I was. It won't happen again", Robert replies as he starts laughing to himself.

As Jimmy was heading down the corridor, he came upon a creature and took it out. Telling Lewis he finds out he is going to go down one of the other corridor's he passed up. "Jimmy. I'm heading down the right one. If you come back then take the one in the middle and I will come back to the central area in 3 hours. Over", Lewis says.

"Okay Lewis. I'm going to keep heading in this direction for a little longer, and then I will come back. Over", Jimmy responds.

"Roger. Out", Lewis says as he heads down the corridor. As it curves slightly to the right, he hears something from up around the bend, but can't quite make it out. Going further down the corridor, it gets louder. As he comes to a split in the corridor, Lewis peers around the edge and takes a look, and sees 10 of the creatures doing what looks like, maybe, eating. Gross.... He thinks as he decides to contact Jimmy and tell him he is going to take out a group of the bastards. "Jimmy. You there?" Lewis asks into his headset.

"Right here. What do you need?" Jimmy replies back.

"I have a group of creatures that are eating....
Or... I guess.... What passes for eating? I am
going to take them out. If you hear me say,
BITCH, then I need your help immediately. Okay?
Over", Lewis tell him.

"Roger. I will be listening. Have fun there
buddy", Jimmy says as he heads down the
corridor he is currently in.

Looking around the corner Lewis times his
surprise attack precisely, as he jumps out from
the corridor and falls flat on his face. As he hits
the ground, his weapon fires and takes out the
whole group. "Damn", he says as he gets up and
sees another group coming down the corridor. As
they see him, they open fire. As he turns around
and fires he hauls ass away from the new group.
As he runs down the hall he looks down the
corridor he is presently in and sees yet another
group, coming towards him. As they see him,
they start firing. As an energy pulse hits the wall
near his face, Lewis ducks down and fires his
weapon. As he pulls the lever, nothing happens.
Oh no... He thinks. "BITCH", he says as he takes
his nozzle out and gets ready to use it.

"I'm on my way, Lewis. Hold out 'til I get there",
Jimmy replies sounding out of breath and so far
away as he runs back down the corridor he came
from.

As Lewis is lying on the floor, the creatures
from behind him come toward him and fire their
weapons. Caught between two groups, Lewis
gets up and opens the nozzle wide open and
starts spraying the group in front of him. As they
fall back from the coldness of the vapors he turns

around and runs straight for the creatures. As he runs for them they seem to be stunned, as if they didn't expect him to run toward them. As he gets to within 15 feet of them, he opens the nozzle up and sprays the entire group and freezes them. Just then, an energy pulse hits his tanks and knocks him to the floor. As he falls he drops the nozzle and falls unconscious.

As Jimmy comes around the corner, he sees a bunch of the creatures around Lewis' prone body on the ground. Running down the hall he opens fire on the creatures. Not having a chance to respond to the energy pulses coming from behind them, Jimmy takes them all out. Kneeling down next to Lewis, Jimmy shakes him.

"Lewis. Come out of it", Jimmy says as he shakes him a little harder.

Blinking his eyes open Lewis responds still a little dazed from being knocked out, "Where am I?" as he tries to sit up.

"We are aboard the big ship… remember?" Jimmy asks.

"Oh. The last thing I remember, is taking out one group with my Freon and getting hit, then falling", he recalls.

"When I got here, you were surrounded by creatures and they were about to pull the plug on your life, until I took them out", Jimmy says. "You can't go around playing dead all the time, Lewis", Jimmy replies as he starts laughing.

Laughing himself, Lewis says, "I try not to fall asleep except in a bed, but I guess the floor looked as good a place to crash as any", as they both burst out into laughter as they both feel as tired as the other.

"Okay. I take it this must be the way to go. Are you ready to go?" Jimmy asks Lewis as he offers him his hand.

"Yeah. That catnap sure rested me right up", Lewis replies as he takes Jimmy's hand and they both start laughing again. Lewis falls back to the floor and pulls Jimmy with him. They both are laughing and lying on the floor. A green energy pulse hits the wall right them. As the sparks tumble to the floor, Jimmy fires off his tanks of Freon towards the creatures attacking them. Lewis rolled over and fired his as well in the same direction. As the vapors clear, they see all the creatures lying down on the floor. They were frozen stiff.

Jimmy looks at them and then says, "Hey. Jam a stick up their butt and you will have an alien ice pop", as he bursts out laughing.

Looking over at him, Lewis bursts out laughing as well. "Stop… stop… stop", he says as he tries to stop.

As Jessica stepped out of the craft two energy pulses strike the pod just above her head. Ducking down and trying to get a fix on the creature, she runs in the creature's general direction, while jumping and rolling as the creature fires at her again. As she comes up from her roll she opens the nozzle wide open and sprays in the direction of the creature. As the creature starts freezing, it stumbles down the steps and fires off a quick burst at Jessica.

Skinning her arm she sprays the creature as it lies on the floor. Grabbing the creature's weapon, she goes to the door and tries to open it. Not being very successful she backs up and fires 3 quick bursts at the door. As the bursts blow the door open she gingerly steps through and looks down the corridor. Not seeing anything she heads down to the left.

As she takes her time going down the corridor, she sees a door open and cautiously peers into the room. Not seeing anything inside she goes in. As she enters she realizes she is in a weapons room. Going over and looking at all the weapons she takes one down. It is a very big weapon, but looks like it is not quite as powerful as she had hoped. Checking it out, she can't figure where the fire mechanism is. Touching a button it fires. As it fires it is blown backward, out of her hands. Leaving a hole big enough for a creature to go through, she decides this is the weapon for her as she straps it over her shoulder for later use. Peering out the door she doesn't see anything around and proceeds the way she was going. As she heads down the corridor she hears a noise and proceeds with caution. As she nears a door, she hears a soft purring sound coming from inside. Looking around the edge of the door, she sees a rather large beast of some kind. As she looks around the door again, the beast pricks its ears up and looks in her direction. Sniffing the air, it starts growling.

Going to the door, it sniffs some more. As it catches a whiff of her scent, it growls rather fiercely and jumps out the door. As it jumps out she fires her weapon at it and the energy pulses don't seem to phase it. It leaps at her as she steps back and grabs her nozzle as she drops the weapon. As the beast lands on her chest and knocks her over, with it on top of her, she brings the nozzle up and sprays it full in the face. Yelping strangely, as its face is frozen it runs down the corridor as the front half of its body goes one way, while the back part tries to go the other way. As she watches it, she feels a sort of sorrow for it. But it lasts only a second as she starts laughing while she watches the beast going down the corridor in that odd way.

Going into the room she looks around and sees what looks like some kind of book. Opening it up, it produces a loud whine. Closing it, the noise stops. Looking some more she finds a map of some type, on some kind of flexible fabric/plastic type of material. There is some kind of planet on it, in the middle, that looks familiar, but not quite like earth. There are strange writings on it that she can't decipher. Rolling it up, she stuffs it down her pants, in the back, under her shirt. Leaving the room, she starts getting some kind of static on her headset. "Hellooooo", she says seeing if she gets a reply.

Not getting anything she heads down the corridor once more. As she proceeds cautiously down the corridor, an energy pulse flies by her, and continues on down the corridor past her. Running away from the person, or thing firing at her, she turns around as her finger slides a control lever up, and fires her big ass weapon. As it fires, it knocks her on her ass. Blowing a hole in the side of the ship she looks out the hole and sees thousands of pods approaching the ship. Oh shit.... She thinks as she starts running down the corridor. As she runs a door opens and she runs right into one of the creatures. As it grabs her, it pulls her inside. "HELP", she says hoping someone can hear her screams. As it throws her on the floor it closes the door and comes over to her.

Taking her weapons away from her, it takes her tanks and then takes all her clothes off. As it comes closer, it has this huge thing hanging down that could be...

Heading toward the center of the ship, Bill and Johnny feel a slight vibration shake the ship. As they come to junctures in the corridor, they take what they hope is the right path. Taking a right, they come face to face with 10 of the creatures that just walked out of a door. Raising his weapon Johnny fires and takes out three as Bill opens his nozzle all the way up and let's them have a taste of instant freeze. "How do you like that", Bill says as he sprays the creatures.

"I think you are losing it buddy", Johnny replies to Bill, as they start laughing.

Going over to one of the creatures Bill picks up one of their weapons and says, "Nice... light... but powerful".

"Okay. Let's get our asses moving. We don't have much time before we get caught, if we are not careful", Johnny says.

Proceeding down the corridor, they take a left and start down a new corridor. As they are going down the corridor, Johnny comes flying by Bill, as he is hit in the back. Landing on the floor in a lifeless pile, Johnny is unconscious. Turning around with rapid reflexes, Bill fires his weapon down the corridor taking out 3 of the creatures. "YOU SON OF A BITCHES", Bill yells as he runs down the corridor making sure there are no more around. Going back to Johnny, he bends down and checks for a pulse. Feeling a slight one he stands guard for a short time. After about fifteen minutes Johnny starts moving and coming to.

"Ohhhhhhhhhhhhhhhh... Shit damn", Johnny says as he leans up on one elbow. "What the hell hit me?' he asks.

"One of those creatures fired at you and hit you from behind. I guess the force of the shot blew you past me", Bill replies as he helps Johnny to his feet.

"Are you okay to travel?" Bill asks Johnny as he shakes his head.

"Yeah. I'll be fine… as soon as this ringing stops. Good thing I had my bullet proof vest on, huh?" Johnny replies.

Heading in the direction they were heading they come to a strange, door type thing. As Bill looks at it, he figures it is 10 feet tall and 15 feet wide. But there aren't any switches or mechanisms that look like it would open it. Just then, the door opens and 30 of the creatures come walking out. Bringing their weapons up, they start firing on the creatures and manage to kill all but three of them. The three they didn't kill ran off down the corridor squealing. "Damn… that was good", Bill says as he jumps inside the doors, before they can close.

Before Johnny has a chance to go through the doors, they close and separate them. "Bill, you there?" Johnny asks into his headset. Getting nothing but static he decides it is too dangerous to wait around here for the doors to open. When they open again, a bunch of those things might come out again. Heading in the direction that they were going, Johnny enters a rather large open area. Seeing what looks like a row of doors, Johnny goes over and sees if he can figure out how to open them. As he searches he pushes buttons and turns knobs, wherever they happen to be. As he pushes a button, 2 doors open simultaneously and a fog-like vapor comes out of one of the doors.

Being the adventurous type that he is, Johnny goes to the door with the fog stuff coming out of it and goes in. As he goes through the door it closes behind him. "Oh damn", Johnny says as he realizes he doesn't know how to get back out. Going forward he looks around and can't see anything because of the fog. As he walks forward, he bumps into something like a glass tube. When he hit the tube-like thing, it cleared a spot on it. Going over to it, he starts rubbing the side of the tube. As he gets a spot big enough to look into it, he looks and sees a human inside, floating in mid air. As his senses take over his body, he moves away from the tube and throws up. As his retching subsides he wipes his mouth off with his arm. Walking away from the tube, Johnny tries to find a way out. Feeling his way around, he feels something, like a button.

Pushing it a door opens and he is in a corridor again. Looking out, before he steps out of the room, he doesn't see any of those creatures around. Just then, he hears a noise coming over his headset. "Hello", Johnny says seeing if anyone is out there.

"Is that you Johnny?" he hears back.

"Yeah. Who is this?" Johnny asks.

"It's Jimmy and Lewis. Where are you?" Jimmy asks.

"I don't know. I just came out of a room for storing humans", Johnny replies.

"What the hell are you talking about?" Jimmy and Lewis ask together.

"There is a room with tubes in it and they are storing humans inside them. I have no idea where I am at", Johnny says.

"Well, hold on. We will see if we can find you. Okay?" Jimmy asks Johnny.

"You got it. I just hope there are no more creatures around though. Hurry it up too", Johnny says as his voice starts to quiver from fear.

Just then, the hand of a creature reaches out and grabs Johnny by the neck. "AHHHHHHHHHHHHHH", Johnny yells as the creature breaks his neck with a snap...CRACKKKK.... Like it was butter. Throwing his body aside the creature heads down the hall looking for more invaders. As the creature is leaving, you can hear Johnny's headset, "Johnny, you still there?" "JOHNNY", Jimmy yells.

# CHAPTER 19

As Stiderion comes out of his bunger, he sees one of the invaders and sneaks up on him. As he reaches out he grabs the human by the neck and squeezes as the human makes some kind of noise. As he hears a crack he throws the human aside as you hear, "Johnny, you still there?" JOHNNY", as he walks down the corridor in search of the other humans. Walking toward command control Stiderion doesn't run into any more humans. As he enters the command control he bows and says, "My Commander Knightwarp, I have a report for you".

"You had better be here to tell me you have killed all the humans aboard our ship. I will accept no less than that… Stiderion", Knightwarp says as he paces and hits the wall every few minutes.

"No, my commander. We have killed all but six of them. We have the others in a trap right now", Stiderion replies as he continues bowing.

"I want all the intruders off my ship by tonight. If not, then it is your heads on the line Stiderion", Knightwarp says in a stern tone. "Now go and finish the task I have set before you", Knightwarp demands as he kicks Stiderion as he walks out.

Walking out he feels the boot of Knightwarp hit him in the ass. Leaving command control he heads in the opposite direction than where his bunger is. As he walks down the corridor he can hear Jinforin blabbing about how he can do anything. Shaking his head he proceeds down the corridor. Taking a chance that the humans might have gotten to the core of the ship, he heads in that direction. Walking down the corridor he sees a gap in the ship up ahead. "Son of a human", Stiderion mumbles as he goes over, and surveys the damage. "This can only have been done with my super-ripper stabilizer gun", he says, "I will get you, whoever has my weapon, "Stiderion says to himself. Walking back the way he came, he takes a detour and goes to the other side of the gap. Taking the corridor that Jessica just went down, not more than 10 minutes ago, he can smell her. Following her scent, he intends on making her pay for what she has done.

While he is walking down the corridor he gets an odd feeling… like he is being followed. Turning around he looks back the way he came and sees a blur cross the corridor. Going back he looks down the corridor and sniffs, trying to see if he can pick the scent out. Not smelling anything different from what he already smelled he guesses it must be the same human who has his weapon. Following where the blur went Stiderion heads down the corridor in search of whatever the blur was. As he heads down the corridor, he notices a door open and goes to close it. As he reaches for the button to close it, he hears the whine of his special weapon. Turning around he looks down the corridor and sees the human with his weapon pointing it at him.

Shaking his head he knows he is done for. Letting out a high-pitched squeal in defeat, he sees her drop the weapon and covers her ears. As he continues making the squeal he heads down the corridor, towards the human. As she covers her ears up, she looks up and sees the creature coming towards her. Not caring about the noise she bends down and picks the weapon up. As she cringes in pain, she fires the weapon at the creature and rips a hole in the ship where the creature was just standing.

# CHAPTER 20

As the creature comes towards her she rolls over and grabs the nozzle of her tanks and squirts the creature right where it counts on a man, hoping that was what that was. As it freezes and it squeals in pain she trains the nozzle on its face and stops the squealing. As it falls down and breaks, she grabs her clothes and tries to make some kind of covering for her body. Making the bare necessities for her body, she puts her tanks back on and grabs up the big ass gun and the other gun. Going into the corridor she turns left and continues on her way. As she walks down the corridor she sees a creature going down the way she had already been. Running across the split in the corridor, she steps inside a small alcove. Just as she got her body into the alcove, the creature comes past her and walks down the corridor. As it passes her she keeps as quiet as she can, not even breathing.

Waiting for 20 seconds she cautiously steps out and sees the creature down the corridor. As she aims her big ass gun down the corridor, towards the creature, she sees it turn and look at her as the whine of the gun grabs its attention. As it faces her it lets out a high-pitched squeal that hurts her ears. As the creature squeals, she drops the big ass gun and covers her ears instinctively. As she looks up, she sees the creature coming toward her. Not caring whether it hurts or not, she uncovers her ears and bends down to pick up the big ass gun. As she aims it at the creature the pain in her head is almost unbearable. Bracing herself for the impact, she fires the weapon and blows a hole in the ship, where Stiderion was.

Going over to the new hole she made, she peers down into it and sees pods all over the place. As she peers out a pod takes a shot at her and burns a hole in the deck next to her. Backing away from the hole she goes back down the corridor she came from. As she passes the room where the creature was going to take her, she shudders. Turning right at the first split, she heads down a new corridor. As she comes to another split, she hears voices coming from around the corner. Cautiously peering around the corner she sees a group of creatures coming her way. Looking for a place to hide, she finds an open door and goes in. As she enters the room the door closes.

Trying to find some kind of switch or something to open the door with, she hears the creatures outside the door. Going to a small vent, she opens it up and climbs in. As she closes the vent, the door opens and the creatures come in. Watching them she decides she wants to see what they do in here. As she watches she sees one sit down in a chair and another one hook up some kind of thing to its head. After it is placed on its head, the other creature goes over to a panel and pushes some buttons and flips some switches. As the creature in the chair starts writhing as if in pain, it lasts only for a few seconds. As each one goes through this procedure, she can't even begin to think what it does. As she waits for the creatures to get done she watches as one of the creatures' opens the door and sees the switch she had been looking for.

As the last creature leaves and closes the door, she comes out of her hiding place and goes over to the switch and is just about to open the door, when it opens by itself. Looking up as the door opens, she sees about 50 of the creatures outside the door. As they see her they come in and try to grab her. As the door opened and she saw all the creatures, she ran over to the vent and got in, just before they could grab her. As she crawls down the vent shaft, she can hear the creatures in the room, squealing loudly. Coming to a junction she goes down one to the right and backs down the one on the left. As she crosses over, she can see the room about 75 feet down the tube. Aiming her big ass gun down the tube, she props it against the corner and fires it.

As the energy ball, (about 2 feet in diameter), flies down the tube it blows out the vent and blows up the room the creatures were in. As she feels the impact, a fireball of flame rushes down the tube towards her. Backing farther into the tube, she can only hope it just keeps going straight. When she is about 15 feet from the junction, she sees the fireball rush past and down the tube. Feeling the heat from the fireball her face feels like it is on fire itself. Touching it she can feel the hotness still there. Wincing as she touches it, she takes her hand away and starts backing down the tube she is in. As she is backing down the tube, she can hear the squealing of one of the creatures. Following the sounds she comes to a vent in the ceiling of this room, where this creature is. As it squeals she feels pity for it. Grabbing her nozzle for nitrogen, she puts the nozzle into the room and squirts it on the creature.

As the creature squeals it stops squealing as soon as the freeze blast does its work and freezes it. "Hello", she says in the hopes that someone is nearby. Hearing nothing but static, she continues down the tube. Coming to a tube that goes down she is about to cross over and keep going, when she notices steps in the side of it. Deciding to go down, she backs up to the steps and places her foot in the first one. As she descends deeper into the ship, she looks down and can't even see the bottom. As she continues to climb she tries her headset again, "Hello... Is anybody there?"

Waiting for a few seconds, she continues on. Climbing down, her arms start to get tired from too much climbing and not enough exercise.

While climbing down she notices another tube that connects to this one. Sliding into the tube she rests for a few minutes as her arms start to feel like she actually has some again. As she waits to get rested, she can only think what everyone else is going through. After about 5 minutes, she gets out of the tube and continues her descent into the heart of the ship. Climbing down again, she feels like she has been climbing for hours. Looking up she sees she has entered a big chamber where all the tubes connect together. Looking down she finally sees the floor. As she gets to within 8 feet of it she drops down and lands on her feet.

Brushing her hair out of her face, she stands and looks for some kind of door.

As Jimmy and Lewis lose contact with Johnny, they continue down the corridor they were heading down. As they walk down the corridor they see a hole up ahead. Looking out the hole, they see thousands of the pods hovering by the ship. As they are looking down, energy pulses hit all around them. As they back up, they go back the way they came and turn left at the next junction. As they are heading down the corridor they hear some kind of a mewling, coming from the end of the corridor. As they get closer, Lewis sees it is some kind of creature. Probably one of the aliens' babies, or maybe it also was another species they had enslaved. Taking aim Lewis shoots it. When the energy burst doesn't do anything to the creature, he grabs the nozzle of his tanks and tries to spray the creature. Pulling the lever, nothing happens. "Oh shit", Lewis says as he grabs Jimmy's arm and tugs at his arm. "Come on. Let's get out of here before it decides to have us for a snack", Lewis says.

"You don't have to tell me twice", Jimmy replies as they head down the corridor from where they came.

Going back the way they came, they take the last corridor they haven't taken yet. As they proceed down the corridor, they meet up with a scout troop, coming in from a docking bay. Shooting them as they come through the door, the last few back up into the dock. As the door closes Jimmy fires at the door and blows it open. As the door flies inward, it takes out 3 of the four creatures. As Lewis steps through the door, he fires at the last one and kills it. "Room clear", he says as they leave and go back into the corridor.

Heading down the corridor they come to a place that they guess, may have been a room, but is now a doorway outside. "Looks like one of our people has been here", Jimmy says.

"Yeah. I just wonder who has something that can do this kind of damage!" Lewis states.

"I don't know, but I just hope it's one of our people that can do this… cause if not… then we are in trouble", Jimmy says as he sees all the pods floating around outside. "Come on. Let's go. Maybe we can catch up to whoever… or… whatever did this", Jimmy says as he grabs Lewis' arm and drags him away from the hole.

Going down the corridor Jimmy sees a troop of creatures coming down the corridor toward them. Looking for a place to hide, Lewis sees a vent and says, "Look. We can go down the ventilation system and maybe get to the core quicker", as he bends down and opens the vent. Climbing in Lewis says, "Come on Jimmy. Before they get here".

"I can't. I'm afraid of small spaces", Jimmy says as a scared look comes over his face.

"Look. It's either you or them. If you die… we may all die. If you face your fear head-on, you can overcome it. Now come on", Lewis tries to goad him trying to talk him into the shaft.

"Okay", as he gets down and gets in.

Backing down the shaft, they come to the same downward tube as Jessica did. Seeing the steps, Lewis backs down them and starts going down. Once he is down a short ways Jimmy backs down and starts down them also. Climbing down, Lewis says, "Is this so bad now?"

"Maybe not. But I still prefer large open spaces", Jimmy replies as they climb down.

As they reach the bottom, they look for a door to go out of. "I wonder how far we came down?" Lewis says more to himself.


When Bill went through the big doors and Johnny didn't make it, he felt the sudden sensation of going up. Riding the lift up he suddenly has this crazy idea that he is going to be ambushed as soon as the doors open. Grabbing another weapon from one of the fallen creatures, he faces out the door and waits to see if anything is on the other side when the doors open. As he feels the movement halt, he prepares himself for a battle. As the doors open he looks out and doesn't see anything. Looking both ways he sees a corridor that looks like it goes around in a circle. Going to the right, he runs right into 2 creatures standing outside a door. As he fires at the creatures they grab for their weapons, but are too late. Bill blows them away and drags their bodies around the corner. He huffs and puffs as he drags them. As he searches for the button or switch the door opens and a creature comes out. As it walks down the corridor away from Bill, it doesn't seem to notice him.

Jumping into the door Bill sees 3 creatures standing at a console and one big mother of a bastard standing in the middle, waving his arms in the air. Not giving the creatures any time to react Bill fires both weapons and takes out all four creatures. Going over to the console that the creatures were around, he looks at it and starts pushing buttons. As he pushes buttons, the ship starts tilting one way, then the other. Other times it feels like it is going higher and then it feels as if it is going lower. Starting to get the hang of it, Bill starts heading forward. As the big ship moves north, it creates waves that start lapping at the bottom of the ship.

Feeling it starting to get sluggish, Bill pulls a lever and it feels like it is rising. As he continues playing with all the controls, he doesn't notice as 2 creatures come in. Seeing him at the console, they open fire and hit Bill in the back. As he falls forward onto the console, his hand hits the lever that takes it down and the ship plunges into the ocean. Going over to the console the creature tries to bring the ship back up. Looking down he

sees Bill setting the timer for the bomb. Smiling
for the last time, Bill looks up and says,
"GOODBYE, BASTARDS", as the bomb explodes
and rips a hole in the center of the ball, at the top
of the ship.

Walking down the corridor, Nick and Robert
see the big holes all over the place. "I wonder
who or what did that?" Robert blurts out as they
come to the first one.

"You got me, but I hope it's on our side", Nick
replies with a smile on his lips.

Heading away from the hole, they take a right
and go down the corridor. As they are going down
the corridor, they hear noises coming from
somewhere up ahead. Putting his finger to his
lips, Nick walks forward as quietly as he can.
Getting to the corner, he peers around. As he
looks, he sees 25 of the creatures, fully armed
and ready for battle. Backing up, he backs into
Robert. Turning around, he whispers, "There are
about 25 creatures and they are fully armed as if
ready for battle. Let's surprise the hell out of them
and"... As the creatures come around the corner
and spot them.

When the creatures spotted them, they started
firing at them. Turning around Nick opens fire with
his weapon and immediately takes out 5 of them.
As Robert takes out 3, the rest fall back behind
the corner. "Watch our backs in case they try to
sneak up on us", Nick tells Robert.

"Okay dude", Robert replies.

Watching behind them Nick runs around the
corner and has his nozzle in his hand, ready to

spray something with it. As he rounds the corner, he sees there is nothing there. Going back he looks for Robert, but he is gone. "Robert. Where the hell are you?" Nick asks.

"I went around the corner when I heard something. Where the hell did you go to, anyway?" Robert asks back.

"I rushed down the corridor where they were at, and when I got there, they were gone. Meet me back where we were, okay?" Nick replies.

"Okay. Be there in a sec", Robert says.

Waiting for Robert to show up Nick sees movement ahead in the corridor. As he looks hard, trying to figure out what it is, Robert comes up and says, "What're you looking at?" as Nick just about jumps out of his skin.

Turning around Nick says, "Don't you ever freakin' sneak up on me. I'm scared enough without you making it any worse".

"Sorry. What were you so intent on down there?" Robert asks as he looks and sees what looks like shadows. "Now I see. Have you figured out what it is yet?" Robert asks.

"Not yet. We will have to wait 'til we get closer", Nick replies as he heads in the direction of the shadows.

Moving toward them, they get farther away. "Wait a minute. I don't like this one bit", Nick says. "I'll be damned if I follow them any longer" as he walks down a different way.

Following Nick, Robert looks back and sees the shadows moving with them, but keeping the same distance. As he keeps looking over his shoulder, Robert gets a strange feeling. "Hey

Nick. Are you getting a strange feeling like you are being watched", Robert asks.

"Yeah. The hairs on the back of my neck are tingling. What do you think we should do?" Nick asks him as they continue to walk.

"I say do what we are doing. It doesn't matter where we go. We can always run into these things, anywhere", Robert says.

Just then, a door opens to Nick's right and out walks a small group of creatures as they are squealing to themselves. Raising his weapon Nick fires and hits the first two. Jumping to the side of the door, Nick grabs the nozzle of his tanks and sticks it in the door and pulls the lever wide open, flooding the room with nitrogen vapors. Pushing the lever back Nick looks around the corner and sees all the creatures frozen solid. Walking into the room Nick looks around and sees some kind of chair, or something and a creature in it, strapped down with something on its head. "Now what the hell do you make of that?" Nick states as Robert came into the room.

"You got me on that. Your guess is as good as mine", Robert responds as he investigates a little closer.

Not seeing anything worth staying for, they go back into the corridor and are under fire as soon as they step into the corridor. Ducking down Nick looks up and fires his weapon. Looking at the weapon, Nick sees a slide control and he slides it all the way up. Firing down the corridor, the gun pushes Nick back as it fires and produces a huge 2-foot ball of energy. Flying down the hall it blows up when it hits a creature that peers around the corner and gets it right between the eyes. Tearing a huge hole in the ship, (not as big as the other holes), Nick goes over and looks out. He sees all the pods still out there, waiting for something. Backing up before one of them starts firing, Nick and Robert head down the corridor the way they were going.

As they round a bend, they enter a huge area. It must be 300 feet high and about a quarter of a mile wide. "This looks like a storage room. I wonder what kind of shit they store here", Nick muses as he goes over and tries to open one of the boxes.

Not getting it open Nick backs up and slides the control to a lower setting and fires it. As the energy pulse hits it, the side falls off and out comes this real big thing. Going over to it Nick looks at it and tries to pick it up. As he lifts it, it feels like it weighs only a few pounds. Robert says, "I guess looks are deceiving, huh", as he smiles.

"Yeah right", Nick replies as he smiles. "I wonder what the hell it is" he muses.

"I don't know. Let's screw with it so we can blow ourselves up though, okay?" Robert says sarcastically as they both burst out laughing.

"Okay. Here, I will push this and see what it does", Nick says as he pushes the button and a red fireball comes out the end and goes about 50 feet, before turning around and coming straight at them.

"OH SHIT", Robert says as he starts running for cover.

"SCREW THE HELL OUT OF ME", Nick says as he sees the fireball heading for him.

Getting up he runs behind a row of boxes. Peering around the corner of the box, it comes flying by, as it makes a sizzling like sound. Pulling his head back Nick heads back to the thing and picks it up. Running to the other side of the room, Nick looks over his shoulder and doesn't see the fireball coming back. "Robert, you there?" Nick asks.

"Yeah. This fireball thing is chasing me. I can't seem to get rid of it", Robert replies as he sounds like he is out of breath.

Going to the boxes he saw Robert go into, he encounters the fireball. Ducking down it sizzles where he was. Looking down the row of boxes, Nick says, "Robert… stay where you're at. I am going to see if it will take out a group of creatures I see, down the row of boxes I am at", as he starts running while the fireball chases him.

"Okay. Good luck", Robert replies.

As Nick darts in and out of boxes the fireball follows him. Dropping the thing Nick runs right at the group of creatures. Looking at him, they draw their weapons. As he is running and only 20 feet away from them, he ducks down and the fireball flies over him. As it flies over his head the creatures see it and try to run, but don't have time. As the fireball hits them, it makes a loud explosion. Looking up, Nick sees all the creatures totally disappear. "WOW", Nick yells out as he watches the fireball do its damage. Standing up, Nick goes back and picks up the thing that created the fireball. Walking back the way he came, Nick finds Robert, hiding in between 2 boxes.

"You are crazy man. I was only joking when I said we should play with it", Robert replies as he stands up.

"I didn't mean to push the button. It just happened. Sorry", Nick says as he tries to look sad, but can only manage to start laughing.

"What the hell is so damn funny?" Robert wants to know.

"I can't help it", as he laughs a little harder. "It was just sort of funny… when it came out the end and you went running, like you saw a ghost or something", Nick says as he burst out laughing again. "I guess I owed you that, for always sneaking up on me".

"Okay. We're even now", Robert replies.

"Yeah… okay", Nick replies. "Now, let's get the hell out of here", as he starts walking in the direction they were headed, before finding the thing.

Walking in between boxes, they come to what looks like some kind of door. Looking around for something to open it with, (a switch or button), Nick pulls a lever and the door opens. Looking inside, it is a small room about 9 feet high and about 8 feet square. As they both go through the door and cross the thresh hold, the doors close. "Oh shit", Nick says as they try to open the doors.

Not having any luck, Robert says, "Man, you are bad luck. Every time you do something, it goes wrong", as he starts smiling.

"Yeah. Well then fine. We can split up", Nick replies as he starts to smile.

As they get the sensation that they are going down, the doors open and there are 3 creatures about to step in, when Robert brings his gun up and fires it at the creatures. Taking them out, some more come around a corner and see them as the doors close. Waving at them, Nick smiles and starts laughing. Getting the feeling that they are going down again, the lift stops and the doors open. Looking out, they see nothing except a huge room, (bigger than the storage place), with all kinds of tubes and pipes everywhere. Hearing a noise come over his headset, Nick says, "Hello. Anyone out there?" as he waits to see if he gets a reply.

"I'm here", Jessica says. "Where are you?" she asks him.

"We just stepped off an elevator or lift, and are standing outside of the doors, right now", Nick replies as he paces the floor.

"I will be there in a minute. I just found something that looks like what we may be wanting", Jessica says as she looks the thing over and walks back to the doors she saw earlier. As she walks out from between two rows of equipment, she sees Nick and Robert and waves at them.

Waving back Nick says, "You look like you have been through hell. What have you been doing, playing again", as Nick and Robert both burst out laughing.

"Hey. I had a hell of a time. After Julio got killed and I was alone, I have been up to my eyeballs in creatures. Can't you tell", she says as she pulls her eyelid down so they can see.

They all start laughing, as she does that. Showing them the way she came from, she shows them what she thinks is what they are looking for. "Hmmm." Nick hums as he looks at it. "I don't know Jesse. It looks good, but I think they would have the vital parts locked up in a secure area", as he continues to look.

"You know. You may be right", Jessica says.

"So let's go find a door that is hard to get into", Robert suggests.

As they walk looking for something to indicate that they are close to the core, Nick asks, "Hey Jesse. Did you see those huge holes that got blown in the ship? Whoever did that has got to have a hell of a weapon".

"That was little old me. I found a weapons room or something and I picked up this baby", she says as she shows them her big ass gun.

"Kewl", Nick says, as he looks it over.

"Score one for our side", Robert replies as he looks it over.

"But have you checked out my recent acquisition?" Nick asks as he shows her the new weapon he picked up in the storage room.

"What does it do?" she asks, as she looks it over.

"I don't really know, except that when I pushed this, a fireball came out and came after us, until I lured it into a group of creatures", Nick says as he points at the button.

"I wonder what else it can do?" Jessica muses.

"I guess we'll find out when the time is right", Nick replies as a smile plays about his lips.

Seeing a huge door straight ahead, Nick points and says, "I guess maybe we are looking for something like that".

"That looks like what we might be looking for", Jessica says as they head for it.

Just then, they start getting something over their headsets. "Hello. Who is this?" Nick asks.

"It's Jimmy and Lewis. Who is this?" Jimmy asks.

"This is Nick, Robert and Jessica. Where are you?" Nick asks back.

"We came down a ladder from a vent and we can't figure out how to get out of here", Jimmy replies as he sounds like he is panicking.

"Oh, that's easy", Jessica says, "Look up to your left when standing in front of the door and there is a lever about 8 feet up. Push the lever up and the door will open", as she explains to them how she did it.

## CHAPTER 21

As Lewis and Jimmy look for something to open the door with, they hear some kind of static coming over the radio. "Hello. Who is this?" they hear.

"It's Jimmy and Lewis. Who is this?" Jimmy asks.

"This is Nick, Robert and Jessica. Where are you?" Nick asks them.

"We came down a ladder from a vent and we can't figure out how to get out of here", Jimmy says as he sounds like he is panicking.

"Oh, that's easy", they hear Jessica say. "Look up to your left when standing in front of the door and there is a lever about 8 feet up. Push the lever up and the door will open", Jessica says as she explains to them how she did it.

Looking up, Jimmy says, "There it is", as he points at it. "I will boost you up and you push the lever up, okay?" Jimmy asks Lewis.

"Yeah… okay", replies as he lifts a foot, waiting for Jimmy.

Boosting him up, Lewis pushes the lever up and the doors slide open. After letting him down, Jimmy runs through the doors with Lewis right behind him. Looking around they see they are in a huge room with tubes and pipes all over the place. "Where are you guys at?" Jimmy asks.

"When you come out of the doors, go to the left and follow that to the big doors that you can't miss. We are at the big doors… we are trying to figure out how to open them ", Jessica tells them.

"Okay. We will be there as soon as we can", Jimmy replies as he leads the way to the left.

Once they see the huge doors, they can see the rest of the attack force looking around. Running to them, Jimmy and Lewis say in unison, "This is the most screwed up ship I have ever been on", as they start laughing.

"I hear you", Nick replies in a sarcastic tone as he adds, "I bet it's the only ship you've been on", as he starts chuckling.

"Come on. We are looking for something that will open this door", Jessica says.

As they look about, hundreds of creatures that are hiding everywhere in the place ambush them. As they all do what comes natural, they avoid the energy pulses and take cover. "This is a fine damn situation", Nick says as he returns fire.

"You aren't telling me anything new", Jessica replies as she fires her big ass weapon and takes out about 15 of the things. "Yahooooooo", Jessica says as the creatures squeal in pain.

Checking out the thing that he is holding, Nick points it at the creatures and upon seeing what he's got, they scatter and run away. Pushing a different button, a 5-foot buzzing energy ball comes out the end and shoots at the creatures. As it flies towards them, it hits a box and takes the corner out. As it continues it hits 5 creature's dead on and explodes in a fiery fireball. As it explodes it takes out a huge contingent of the creatures. It also blew a hole the size of an 18-wheeler semi. The ones it didn't get ran out of there.

"BITCHIN' GUN", Nick yells out as he looks back at the door that they can't seem to open.

"Now that is what I call firepower", Jessica says as she starts laughing.

"Hey, Jesse. You think this thing will take out the door?" Nick asks.

"I don't know. Why not find out", Jessica replies.

"Oh sure. Leave it to Mr. Badluck there", Robert says as him and Nick start laughing together.

"Here goes nothing", Nick says as he aims and pushes the same button, or so he thinks. As it fires, a small ball of energy comes out the end, and starts toward the door. As it hits, it burns a hole clean through it. "I wonder what the hell that was" Nick muses.

"I guess that will do", Jessica says as she starts towards the hole in the door.

As they climb through the hole, they see a row of massive blocks. They are about a city block in diameter and have all kinds of tubes and pipes and wires leading from them. "That must be what we are looking for", Jessica says.

"Yeah. But how the hell do you take out all of those, with just a few small bombs?" Jimmy asks.

"I'll show you how", Nick replies as he puts his finger on the one button that produces the huge energy ball.

Going to the end of the room, he aims the thing at the first one and fires it. As the ball of energy comes out of it, it heads straight for the massive block and takes it out, throwing debris everywhere. Ducking as he tries to avoid being hit, Nick hides behind a row of boxes that are near at hand. As the debris stops falling, he looks out and sees he took out the whole block. "DAMN, NOW THAT'S WHAT I CALL SERIOUS FIREPOWER!" Nick yells out as he observes the damage.

"Oh shit", Jimmy says. "Now… we have created a monster", Jimmy replies as everyone starts laughing.

Going to the next one, Nick hides before firing it again. As he fires it another block is destroyed. As debris rains down all around Nick, a big piece of the block comes and lands on his legs, breaking them, as he hears the crunch of bones being smashed. "AHHHHHHHHHHHHHH", Nick yells out in pain.

Going over to him, they all try to lift the piece of block off him, but can't seem to budge it. "Go on. Set your bombs for 3 hours and get the hell out of here. When you leave, I am going to fire off as many of these as I can and take out all the shit I can. Now go", Nick says.

"Who made you the leader?" Jessica replies. "We are going to get you out of here. We have lost enough people already", as she states facts.

"I am useless now. Go. I will do whatever it takes to take this ship out. Now go and quit arguing", Nick demands, as he winces as the pain starts throbbing, with a mind of its own.

"Nick. It's been nice knowing you and fighting at your side. Take care", Robert says as tears form in his eyes.

"Nick. I can't leave you here", Lewis says. "You have been the best friend I have ever had... and I don't think I can just leave you here to die alone", he says as he starts crying. "You just don't seem to understand, you mean a lot to me. You are the only true friend I have ever had and to lose that, it's like dying myself. I will stay here with you", he says as he gets a stern look on his face.

"No Lewis... you need to go on and tell everyone what happened here. What if you are the only one that survives? Then the world will have to know what happened here. The more people that go out and tell the story, then the more alert the people will be in the future. Besides... you still have to take out the doorway", Nick replies as he cries himself, not wanting to leave the world like this.

"Okay... but everyone will know what a hero you were and how you took out the big ship by yourself. You will always be remembered as the one guy who saved the planet from annihilation. Take care and say hi to me every now and then, as you always said, you were going to come back as a ghost", Lewis says as he bends down and hugs Nick bye forever.

"And I am not a hero, damn it. I am just a regular guy, who had help saving the planet from invaders", Nick replies as he winces in pain.

As everyone else hugs him or shakes his hand, they go set their bombs around the first block. After they are done, they leave with their shoulders slumped, a much saddened group than what came to the ship. As tears fill his eyes, he waits 'til they have gotten through the door and he starts firing at the rest of the blocks. As he takes out 2 more, the ship starts to shudder and shake. Firing again he takes out another of the blocks and that is when another piece falls down and crushes him, killing him instantly.

As the group left, they were very sad to have to leave him behind like that. Walking with their shoulders slumped… they drag ass to the lift. As they get in and the doors close, they feel the ship shake and shudder. "I guess he is taking the rest of the blocks out", Lewis says as tears well up in his eyes again.

As the lift comes to a stop, they get ready to fire just in case there are some creatures out there waiting for them. As the doors open, they are amazed to see the corridor empty. Stepping out of the lift, Jimmy motions for Jessica and Robert go to the left ahead and he motions that him and Lewis are going to the right. Nodding in agreement, they proceed forward. As they get ready to look around the corner of the junction, the ship shakes violently and they all fall down in the corridor. As Jimmy and Lewis fall down in the junction, they see a group of the creature's fall a little ways down the corridor. Bringing his weapon up, Jimmy fires it 4 times and takes out the group that he was firing at. As Jessica fell backward, Robert fell forward and his gun fired accidentally and took out one creature down the other corridor. Leaning up on one elbow, Robert fires a few more times and takes out the group down his corridor.

"That was close", Robert says as he stands up. "I take it, that Nick is doing his part to take out the ship".

"Yeah. I would guess that is what the shaking is from", Jessica agrees.

As they head in the direction they think is right, they walk down the corridor. As they are walking, the ship is constantly shaking and vibrating. "I think we had better make tracks and fast", Jessica says as she starts running down the corridor. As they run after her, they pass a hole that is down one of the other corridors. Running over by it, Jimmy sees the ocean coming up the ship. As he turns around and runs after the others, he tells them, "We don't have much time people. The ship is sinking into the ocean. I figure… at the rate we are going down, we have about 25 minutes to get out of here, before we sink with it", Jimmy tells them as he keeps running trying to catch up to them.

"Like we needed to know that", Jessica replies.

"I just thought you might want to know and not be surprised by it", Jimmy says as he sounds a little defeated.

"Damn", Jessica says. "I can't remember where I docked at. All these corridors look the same to me", she says as she stops and tries to figure out where they are at.

"Let's just run and look in all the doors we come to", Robert suggests. "We don't have much time and as long as we are moving, we have a chance to find a dock".

"Okay. Let's go this way", Jessica says as she heads down a corridor.

Following her, they encounter quite a few creatures trying to leave the ship. Taking them out as they encounter them, Lewis suggests, "Hey Jessica. Use your big ass gun and blow a hole in the side of the ship. Maybe we can get our bearings from that".

"Okay. Hold on everyone… Stand behind me and hold me up. When I fire this baby, it likes to knock me on my ass", she says as she points it down the corridor they just came from and fires. As it goes down the corridor, it hits the side of the ship and blows a huge hole in the side. Going down to the new hole, they look out and see they still have to go up 3 levels to get to the docking bays.

"Damn. I'm not sure if we will make it", Jessica replies as she backs away from the hole.

As Lewis looks out the hole, he sees all the pods leaving and heading to shore. "Hey guys. All the pods are leaving and heading to the shore", he says.

"Oh great", Jessica says, "That's all we need. Find a dock and no pods. That's our luck", sounding defeated.

"Hey. We have to have better luck now. I mean look at it. Nick isn't here anymore", Robert replies as they all start laughing and then tears come to their eyes, as they remember what he did for them.

"Let's go", Jessica says as she heads down the way they were going.

As they head down the corridor, they run into a rather large group of creatures. As they prepare to fire on them, the creatures fire first and hits Jimmy in the leg. "DAMN", Jimmy says as he grimaces in pain.

"Jimmy's hit", Jessica says. "Cover me. I'm going to get him", as she runs out and grabs hold of Jimmy's arms, and drags him to cover.

# CHAPTER 22

As she gets him around the bend in the corridor, Jimmy says, "Leave me here. I will take out the ones that try to follow you. Go".

"We are not going to leave you. We left behind someone already and we are not about to lose someone else... just because an energy pulse hit him. You can't get rid of us that easily", Jessica says as a slight smirk plays about her lips as they quiver.

Lewis and Robert are firing back, as the creatures start coming forward.

"Jessica", Lewis says.

"Yeah", she replies.

"Fire your big ass down the corridor and take out the creatures", he says as an energy pulse hits the wall... just over his head.

Aiming her big ass weapon down the hall, she fires it and nothing happens. "DAMN", she says as she throws the weapon down. Grabbing her Freon nozzle, she runs right at the creatures as they stand there stunned, not believing that a human would actually try to come at them. As she gets to within 14 feet, she pulls the lever and sprays all the creatures freezing them where they stand. "YEAH", Jessica says as she balls her hand into a fist and pulls her elbow down.

Going back to the group, they help Jimmy up as he limps down the corridor. Seeing a door up ahead, Jessica runs to it and looks for the thing that opens it. As she looks she notices a button at the top and pushes it. As the door opens, they see the ocean creeping up the side ship. "Oh shit. Close it quick", she says.

Reaching up Robert pushes the button and the door closes. As they continue down the corridor, they come upon numerous doors, but none that are worth going into. Turning to the right at the next junction, Jessica sees a row of doors up ahead. Once they get there, they all start looking for a button or something. As they search, a group of creatures comes from one of the doors as it opens. Without warning Jimmy fires on the creatures and takes them out. "Son of a bitch, that was close", Jimmy says as he leans against the wall.

As they all go through the door, they notice they are standing in a small compartment, about 9 feet high and 8 feet square. "Okay. Everyone… get ready in case there is some of those things waiting for us", Jessica states as the ship rocks violently, pushing everyone to the right side of the compartment.

As it starts rocking the other way, they all fall against each other again, the movement of the lift stops. "SHITDAMN", Lewis says. "Is there a hatch or anything up top?" he asks everyone.

Looking up Robert sees a small panel in the ceiling that is probably an access door. "Lewis... Give me a boost. Let me see if I can open that panel up, up there", Robert says as he points to the door.

"Okay", as he kneels down by Robert and cups his hands. "Ready?" Lewis asks. Robert nods and he lifts him up to the door.

As he searches for something to open it with, he notices a small button the same color as the rest of the ceiling and pushes it. As he pushes it, the door slides open. Reaching up through it, he climbs up through the door. "Okay. Let's go", Robert says as he reaches down and grabs Jimmy's hand and pulls him up through the door. Reaching down, Robert helps Jessica next and then Lewis. Once they are up in the shaft, they look up and see wires and cables and a very long climb up. "I hope you all are fit to climb for a while", Jessica says as she mumbles, "Cause I sure as hell ain't".

"What was that?" Jimmy asks as he raises an eyebrow and looks at Jessica smiling.

"Nothing", she says as she grabs a wire and starts climbing up.

"Hey guys. Why don't we just use the ladder in the side of the shaft", Lewis replies as he points at the steps.

Laughing… they all go over and start climbing up. When they get about 200 feet up, a violent explosion rocks the ship and almost pulls everyone free of the ladder. "Hurry up, people",

Jessica says, "I think our bombs just went off and we probably don't have as much time as we once did", as the adrenaline rush she is feeling takes effect.

Coming to a door, Jessica looks for the way to open it and sees a switch on the side. Flipping it, the door opens and she steps out. "Come on. I think this is it", Jessica says as she helps everyone else.

As they all are standing in the corridor, the ship starts rocking violently again as it knocks them all to the floor. As they get up, Robert and Lewis go over to Jimmy and help him up. As they power-walk, (what else can you call a fast walk), they see a door up ahead. As Jessica gets to it, she opens it and sees 1 pod there. "This way", she says as they come up to the door. Going in, the door closes and they get into the pod. As Robert takes the controls he lifts off and takes them out of the dock.

Flying towards land, (or so they hope), Robert flies it like a pro. As they get within sight of land they hear a huge explosion from behind them. Turning the craft around, they all see the big ship disintegrate right before their eyes. Then they see a huge wave of flame coming at them, and fast. Turning the pod back around, Robert flies as fast as he can. Turning around occasionally, he turns once and sees the flame almost on top of them. "Hang on", Robert says as he takes the pod down into the water. As they enter the water they are thrown around as the blast wave hits the pod, just as it hits the water.

## PART III
## JANUARY 5, 2013

# CHAPTER 1

As Robert tried to get the pod to go up, it wouldn't do anything. "I'm not getting any response from the controls", Robert says as he starts panicking.

"Open the door", Jessica says.

Reaching for the button that operates the door, Lewis pushes it but nothing happens. "It doesn't work. Someone get over here and help me get the door open", Lewis says.

"Let's see if we can pry it open", Jimmy replies as he gets to his feet and goes to the door.

"Wait a minute. Stand back", Lewis says as he points his weapon at the door and fires. Nothing happens. "What the...."He starts to say.

"Weapons check people", Jessica says.

Checking his, Robert finds out his doesn't work either. "Mines dead", Robert says.

"Mine's dead too", Jimmy says as he tries to fire it and nothing happens.

"What the hell do we have left?" Jessica asks.

"We have 2 tanks with liquid nitrogen in them. That's it. Let's think people", Robert says.

"Why not try and freeze the door and see if we can break it open", Lewis suggests as he shrugs as they all look at him like he is crazy.

"What the hell", Jessica replies. She grabs a tank and points the nozzle at the door and starts spraying the nitrogen at it.

"Look. It's starting to move", Jimmy says as he moves away from the moving door.

"Yeah, but not the way we want it to move", Lewis observes as he backs away also.

"Quick… someone… grab the other one and start spraying with me", Jessica says.

Grabbing the other tank, Robert starts spraying the door also. Pretty soon, it is pure white and it is colder than the North Pole inside the pod as everyone starts shivering from the cold nitrogen. Throwing his tank at the door, it breaks into a million pieces as the tank goes through the door. "I knew it would work", Lewis says as he smiles.

"Yeah… sure you did", Jessica says as she jumps out and into the ocean. "It looks like we are only a few hundred feet from shore", she states as she starts swimming to shore.

As Jimmy jumps out, he climbs up on top of the pod and hopes he can get closer to shore before having to get into the water. "Hey… Jimmy… come on", Jessica says as she swims away.

"No way. If I jump in, I will attract sharks long before I get to shore. I will wait and see if the pod will float closer first", Jimmy says as he looks around the water.

"Then I will wait with you", Jessica replies as she swims back to the pod and climbs up with Jimmy.

"Hey. What's going on?" Lewis asks as he jumps into the water and climbs up on the pod too.

"Why don't we push the pod in? Three of us should be able to float it close enough for Jimmy to get to shore safely", Robert suggests as he jumps out and swims to the front of the pod and starts pushing it toward shore.

"Come on Lewis", Jessica says as she jumps into the water and helps Robert.

Lewis jumps in and helps. After about 30 minutes, they get about 50 feet from shore. "Okay Jimmy. You should be able to make it now", Jessica says as she swims the rest of the way to shore and flops down on the sand once she gets there.

Jimmy jumps in and swims to the shore and flops down next to Jessica as he says, "Thanks Jesse. I owe you one".

"Okay. I will take you up on that… sometime soon", she says as she starts laughing.

As Lewis and Robert get to shore they both lie down and try to catch their breath. "Now what do we do?" Robert asks.

"I guess we clean up the mess the creatures made of our planet. We need to take it back", Jessica says smiling a very wicked smile.

"Well.... I guess we can do that, if we can figure out where we are", Lewis replies as he rolls over onto his back.

"Okay everyone. We need to find somewhere to sleep for tonight and get rested up, cause who knows how many of those creatures are left", Jimmy says as he rubs his leg.

As they rest up, they fall asleep on the beach. As Lewis wakes up a few hours later, he looks out at the ocean and scans the horizon. Not seeing the green glow anymore he says, "Hey everyone. Wake up", as he shakes everyone awake. "Look. The glow is gone. Maybe that means the doorway is closed", he says excitedly as he goes around hugging everyone and laughing, "We have won"...
OR DID THEY?

Terrence D. Astleford

## ABOUT THE AUTHOR;
Terrence Dean Astleford was born on July 28 in Grand Rapids, Michigan. He currently resides in Florida where he continues writing more stories and working.